1

Somewhere in the distance a nuclear bomb detonated. It was a bomb that had lain silent for over two hundred years, since the Mega-War that had destroyed civilisation on Earth. A few times a year unexploded bombs went off and reminded us of a time we all wanted to forget.

The ground rippled, then settled back in place, like a carpet which had been picked up at one end and was shaken out. Instant dust devils squirted upward across the dusty landscape. The sky wrinkled and caused the wispy clouds to wave like long pieces of gauze. Gradually the distant nuclear thunder faded into the horizon.

The pack of Emmonics we were keeping watch over froze. Their god Blasteron had just given them his mighty approval; the explosion was his roar of delight. Knowing their god was pleased, the Emmonics howled with righteous frenzy and resumed their hunt with even greater determination.

The horde of about fifteen lunatics in white sheets was within ninety feet of running down their most hated foe, known to them only as the Blasphemer. They swiped the air with their gleaming meat cleavers, making a ringing sound as stinging bits of airborne dust clanged onto the glinting blades.

"That is him, isn't it?" Kivi, my female companion asked with disbelief. "That is Reggie Trimagien they're chasing."

"Couldn't be anyone else. Look at the limp, blue skin and that wild purple hair."

"Yep, it's Reggie all right."

"Better signal Ty so the others can come help him."

"Right."

I sprang onto a nearby pile of debris left over from a ruined building and waved toward Ty who was in the van with the others about a mile away.

Ty's special physical feature was his telescopic vision. From a mile away he could see me as clearly as a pitcher sees his catcher from the pitcher's mound.

In this age almost everyone was born with a so-called defect. We regarded them as beneficial features, good attributes to have. Each of the players on the baseball team I was batboy for was born with a special feature which gave him an advantage playing at his particular position.

My friend Kivi – our ball girl and cheerleader – was born with specialised feline-like feet, and speed to match. She could easily race across the hard sand and sometimes razor-sharp ground without cutting or bruising her furry, padded feet.

In this age, no one was really physically deformed because we were all physically deformed. It was the normal condition of the times.

Most of us had twin brothers or sisters, too, because multiple births were the norm. Single births were very unusual. This was nature's way of trying to quickly repopulate the Earth. Unfortunately, few families survived and most of us – like Kivi and I – had lost our identical other halves. Families were attacked by either roving packs of mutated animals, by the Emmonics, or by bands of crevice-cannibals who hunted every living thing, not just other humans.

My family was attacked by a pack of scarp dogs when I was very little. I was only able to escape because of my amazing springing ability. A special group of tendons in my knees let me spring enormous distances to any direction – even backwards and upwards – within seconds. I was uncatchable. Since I had no one left of my family to tell me about my personal history I could only guess at things like my age – between 17 and 20 – and other pieces of my identity. My given name was Kalld; but the baseball players that adopted me just called me Springer because of my special ability of sudden movement.

The white passenger van bounded across the rugged ground to where we were. It carried four members of the Birdperch Radiants baseball team: Ty, the player/ manager, Proof the centerfielder, Ulfson the first baseman and Gelp our catcher. The other players were on another van, heading toward the town where we were supposed to play our next series of games. We weren't really sure where they were and just hoped that they'd join us as planned.

The van skidded to a swerving stop near my perch and the four players leapt out, a couple of them carrying bats as weapons. All of us wore baseball uniforms of one form or another even when we weren't on the field because they were actually best suited for the post-war environment.

"Good work, Springer!" Ty called to me as he led the others toward a confrontation with the Emmonics. "You too, Kivi."

"That's Reggie out there they're chasing," I shouted.

"Let's go, guys!" yelled Ty. "We can't let 'em carve up Reggie. He might be the only hope this planet has."

I bounded back to the van, snatched a bat from the outside rack and carried it back to the scene of the fight, poised nearby if needed. I had been instructed by Ty to keep clear of any serious fighting until I came of age, and he would tell me when that would be. I followed his orders; he was the manager. Kivi was under the same orders.

I was allowed to take part in baseball rhubarbs, however. These were your typical fights between teams which usually consisted of pushing and tugging and rolling around on the ground.

There was one rhubarb that was an exception, though. That was when we played a team from Northern Illinois all of whose players were Neandertal-like of build. For some reason, the people in that area had all developed along caveman lines. Anyway, we got into a rhubarb with that team which became so serious that we eventually had to escape in our van.

But the battle we now faced was a lot more serious. The Emmonics finally caught up with Reggie and he collapsed. A couple of the madmen loomed over him, cleavers ready to fall. That's when our bear-like catcher Gelp put a halt to everything with his booming voice.

"Hey! Get away from him!" he roared like a giant berrup. "Or I'll yank you apart piece by piece and make you dinner for my clan!"

The Emmonics were paralysed with terror. They turned from their victim and gaped at Gelp, their eyes dancing with dread.

Gelp was doing a frightening imitation of a crevice cannibal. These were the semi-human creatures who roamed the desolated countryside in search of any living being – any living being – to kill and eat on the spot.

What made them doubly horrifying was that they always travelled in packs and could appear out of nowhere, suddenly arising from unseen crevices that were hidden all over the landscape. Their skin was armour plated and their two inner fingers were flesh-tearing talons. Even the Emmonics did not risk fighting with them.

Despite the earlier urging of their god Blasteron, the horde of Emmonics chose to flee instead of fight. They probably thought that the crevice cannibals – assuming that's what we were - would devour Reggie anyway and get rid of him for them.

Gelp pretended to run after the Emmonics as they fled. Once they'd gotten far enough away, Gelp returned to where we'd gathered around Reggie who lay exhausted, his blue skin powdered whitish with the dust from the stones.

"Home...home," gasped Reggie, pointing into the distance.

We all looked toward the direction in which he was pointing. Only Ty with his telescopic vision was able to see anything other than a rubble strewn landscape.

"Think you can carry him for a while, Gelp?" Ty asked the catcher.

"Sure, if I knew where I was carrying him to."

"There's a place out there all right – dug into the ground."

Gelp bent over and picked up Reggie, muttering, "I sure wish you could spot melted down cities that easy."

Gelp was a collector. He collected the remains of cities and towns which had been melted into slag heaps by the force of multiple nuclear detonations. That was all that was left of some cities after being hit by several atomic bombs, a tree stump like slag of solidified molten material.

Gelp always fondly remembered the day when we fought the Neandertals in Northern Illinois because it was while we were fleeing in our van that he picked up the slag-heap remains of what had been Joliet. It is still one of the biggest cities in his collection.

The remains of most cities, however, had simply been tossed over the landscape as tons upon tons of highly irradiated debris. It was the weight of this rubble which kept civilisation from growing again.

The Emmonics worshiped and protected the ruins created by the Mega-War. Not only that, they somehow drew nourishment from the radiation stored in the debris, having become a new species of human being.

From horizon to horizon spread the debris, shimmering in the always searing sun. The Mega-War had left us a stark world in many ways. There was only good and bad; monsters and comic book like perils. There were no longer any pressing political or moral philosophies to consider, just a struggle to survive and to spread whatever was left of civilisation.

Everyone had been assigned his portion of the world by the bombs and that is where most people stayed – to live or die there. The travelling baseball teams were the only contact one group of survivors had with another on anything close to a regular basis. Even after more than two centuries.

Our group trudged onward about a quarter of a mile before coming to a slit opening in the ground. It was a flight of stairs which led to Reggie's underground home, a place that had once been a cafeteria.

"You may put me down now," Reggie said in an insulting way.

"Be glad to."

Gelp dropped him not too gently to his feet.

Reggie started down the stairs with a sideways gait due to his deformed leg. One was about five inches longer than the other.

"We have to hurry," Reggie warned us as we followed him. "The Emmonics know that I live here now. They'll be coming back en mass."

Ty turned to Gelp. "How about staying up there at the top of the stairs and keeping lookout for any Emmonics coming our way?"

"Be glad to, Ty. I don't like closed in places anyway."

The rest of us followed Reggie into the cafeteria. At the bottom of the stairs Reggie flicked a wall switch which set the interior aglow with dazzling light. The light burst from a wall-sized mirror that was opposite the stairs and was the purest radiance I ever saw.

"That's not electric light, is it?" asked our centerfielder, Proof.

"No, it's indirect sunlight that I beam down from the surface by using a series of mirrors," Reggie told him. "The mirrors I use down here magnify the light they catch."

"What about at night, or during cloudy days?" Proof quizzed.

"Then I use artificial light. The power comes from a generator that runs on stored solar energy."

Reggie pointed toward a pair of swinging doors which led to what formerly had been a kitchen.

"I prefer the natural light," Reggie continued. "It leaves deep shadows along the edges and in the corners of the room where I can hide and adjust my mind."

We all exchanged bewildered glances. Reggie had the reputation of being not only a super genius but also a highly eccentric one. He seemed to be bearing that out but fortunately he didn't give any signs of being violent.

We followed him farther into the cafeteria. It was a very spacious room with a low ceiling. Most of the tables had been shoved back against the walls and was where Reggie conducted his various scientific experiments. Beakers and alembics and test tubes were all over the place.

But one of the things I liked best about the old cafeteria was the floor. It was made up of tiny, one inch square tiles that were of a light green colour. I can't say why I liked those tiles so much, just that I did.

Reggie walked over to what used to be a group of steam tables which in former days had been used to keep food warm. He began to quickly remove long sheets of blue-gray, silvery speckled material from them.

"I have to hurry and take as many of these as I can," said Reggie. "Now that the Emmonics have found me, this place will never be safe."

"What are those things, anyway?" Proof asked, clanging the leg of the steam table with the bat he'd brought down with him.

"You wouldn't understand."

Proof choked with rage. The reason we called him Proof was because he styled himself an expert about everything, and usually he did have the right answers about many problems. Whether he was really right or wrong, however, he had the ego of a genius who knew he was always right.

"I wouldn't understand!" howled proof. "Did you ever think that someone else might be just as damned smart as you!"

"No! Such a ridiculous thought would never occur to me."

Proof spun toward Ty. "He's crazy! Why'd you let him lead us down here into this death trap?"

"No, I don't think you're right," Ty told him.

I decided to ask a question – maybe the one that should have been asked in the first place. "What is that material used for, Reggie?"

He answered as he packed the large, carpet-like sheets into a metal suitcase like container. "I'm taking care of the world's salvation."

Maybe I should have asked a different question after all. So I did. "How are you planning to save the world?"

"What's the greatest problem we all face?"

"Starvation. Famine."

"Right. And why is that?"

"Because most of the ground that isn't covered with debris is contaminated."

"Right," beamed Reggie. "And these sheets I'm packing away will solve that problem."

Proof re-entered the discussion, snorting, "Those four by six sheets are going to save the world! Ha!"

"They're actually five by five. And yes, these will be able to solve the problem of the debris – by burning it away. Any type of debris."

Our first baseman, Ulfson, finally broke his silence from where he sat with his overly long left arm dangling onto the floor. "That could work. Could really work. But how can those sheets burn hot enough to melt rock and metal?"

"Don't worry. They will. I've already tested them. They're activated by contact with the radiation in the air and will get as hot as the core of a nuclear explosion. Once they start burning they'll go through about ten feet of debris before burning themselves out. But all I have are these ten prototypes. We'll have to make a lot more of them. And a lot bigger, too."

Gelp's deep voice intruded on the conversation from the top step. "Emmonics! Coming from all directions – right toward us!"

"Come on down, Gelp," Ty called.

"Good idea not trying to escape that way," Reggie said. "They'd run us down on the surface in no time."

"Yeah, but we're trapped down here!" cried Proof.

"No we're not. I've got an emergency exit we can use. I know that they haven't found it."

"Shouldn't we be getting to that exit?" Ty said.

"In a moment," Reggie replied, closing the lid of the metal case. He then opened a cupboard door and removed a backpack from it.

"What's that?" Kivi asked with her squeaky voice.

"It's filled with nutrient pills, grenades, fire-starters...things like that. I don't expect to ever come back here."

Reggie then bent over and tugged a cord on a generator, telling us, "This will give us light in the escape tunnel."

Fitted with his backpack and lugging the metal case in his left hand, Reggie led us through the kitchen toward his secret exit. We followed him past walk-in freezers, smaller coolers and various other appliances toward what seemed to be a stainless steel wall.

Reggie gave a slight nudge on the wall at the right spot and it pushed inward, revealing the escape tunnel. We started forward but didn't get far. The escape tunnel we'd been relying on had caved-in and was completely impassable.

"Must've been caused by that nuclear detonation we heard a little while ago" Ty observed. "Caused just enough of an earthquake to bring down the ceiling."

"Well, there's only one way out now," said Reggie, hobbling back into the cafeteria.

As we walked back through the kitchen, Ty snatched a meat cleaver from where it hung on a wall. "Better get some weapons," he said, "and at least try to make a fight of it."

The rest of them grabbed various types of cutlery for weapons. Not me. I picked up a heavy, steel meat tenderiser because it looked like a mace like those used in Medieval times.

"Ha!" remarked Reggie about my weapon. "A thinking man's choice."

His approval felt good to me. It felt even better because I noticed the sneer it caused Proof to toss my way. Kivi winked at me with delight. She and I shared everything; two young people in an adult world. Although we weren't really related, we really acted like brother and sister. We never knew which was the older or younger.

Our group marched to the bottom of the stairway. Just as we started upward, a powerful explosion from the top of the stairs blew us all backward and onto the floor. Tons of stone and debris crashed down the stairway, entombing us in the cafeteria.

2

A dusty sprinkling of light fell from above through the tiny circular opening in the roof. It was an airshaft and had remained unblocked. Of course, it was too small for us to escape through.

"Is everybody all right?" Ty asked.

Voices and movement came from points throughout the room in answer. Everyone was all right.

"So much for your plan to save the world!" Proof snapped at Reggie. "If it weren't for you we'd never have gotten trapped down here."

Gelp was angry, too. But not at Reggie. He was angry at the Emmonics. Our mighty catcher hefted up a huge chunk of concrete and flung it against the wall in fury. He had the strength of ten men, although his disposition was normally very mild.

I crawled over the pile of rubble to where Kivi lay to check on her. She was unhurt and was looking up at the shaft of light seeping from above.

"At least the Emmonics won't chop us up with their meat cleavers," Kivi observed.

"I guess that's one way of looking at it," noted Ulfson, yanking the baseball bat out from under the debris.

"The game's not over till the last out," said Ty.

"You've got an idea?" Proof asked.

"Maybe." Ty stood up and placed himself directly below the hole in the ceiling.

"It lets the fresh air in," said Reggie. "I prefer it to the air conditioning.

"How long is that shaft?" Ty asked.

"I don't know for sure. I never measured it."

"What's your guess."

"About ten feet."

Both Ty and Reggie stood below the hole in the ceiling and stared up into it.

"What would happen if one of your sheets of material was placed outside on the roof above us?" Ty asked.

"The radiation in the air would make it start burning and it would consume whatever is beneath it."

Proof went over to them. "Just how do we get a piece of his material up there? We're down here?"

Ty turned to Ulfson. "Bring me that bat, will you, Ulfson."

Now Ulfson joined them, giving Ty the bat.

"We could lightly wrap one of Reggie's sheets around the barrel of the bat and shove it up the hole."

"Hey!" said Gelp. "That could work!"

"Yeah, but the bat's only about four feet long," noted Proof. "And the shaft is about ten feet long. Where do we get the extra six feet?"

"Ulfson's left arm is about five feet long," Ty replied.

"What if we made the bat a little longer by attaching something to it like one of those table legs?" I suggested.

"That's a great idea!" said Reggie. I've got some strong tape that could join them real tight!"

While Gelp went over to snap off a table leg, Reggie loped over to one of his cabinets and withdrew a roll of heavy black tape.

"If any of this works," said Ulfson, "and the stuff above us starts to burn it's going to get awfully hot down here."

Returning with the tape, Reggie replied, "Right, it'll climb to about 800 degrees Fahrenheit."

"This sounds more like a suicide plan than an escape attempt," remarked Proof.

"Yeah, maybe my idea wasn't that good after all," Ty added.

"Don't worry, our plan will work," Reggie told us, handing the tape to Kivi so that she and I could attach the table leg to the bat.

"I don't see how," Proof groaned.

"The freezers," Reggie answered him as he walked toward the kitchen. "I'll start all of them running at full blast and we can use them for shelter from the heat. We'll only need about five minutes of protection. The sheets will be done burning by then and the heat will escape through the hole in the ceiling. I hope."

As he entered the kitchen to fire up the freezers Kivi and I did the taping job. We soon had an eight foot extension, including baseball bat, ready to be thrust up the air shaft.

Reggie returned to the main room. Everyone gathered beneath the air shaft with Ty directing operations.

Reggie removed a sheet from his metal container and gave it to Ty who draped the material over the barrel of the bat. He handed Ulfson the bat.

"Hey Gelp," Ty said, "how about lifting Ulfson up toward the ceiling so he's closer to the shaft and will have even more length to his arm?"

"Right. Good idea."

Gelp joined his hands together and made a step for Ulfson. The long-armed first baseman put his right foot into Gelp's hands and stuck the bat up the air shaft at the same time that he was heaved upward.

When he was lowered back down it was with a naked bat, having deposited the flammable material onto the outside roof.

Reggie turned and hobbled toward the kitchen, saying, "Follow me. Hurry!"

We rushed behind him into the kitchen. Each of us found a large, walk-in stainless steel freezer and opened the door. Damp, slightly cool air wafted out; not nearly cold enough.

"I hope you don't think that this is cold," Proof said to Reggie.

"What! The freezers were working a second ago."

"They ain't now," noted Ulfson.

"It already feels like a hundred degrees in here," I observed.

Gelp – who was our mechanical expert – studied the situation. "Well," he said, "the lights in here are still on which means that the generator's giving out enough power. There must be a short or break in the main wire to the freezers."

The sound of the cafeteria's ceiling liquefying urged us to quick action.

Gelp dropped to his knees near the generator and examined the heavy electrical cords. I fell beside him to help.

"What am I looking for?" I asked.

"Any kind of tear or break in the skin of the wire."

"Right."

The others stood near their chosen freezers, slumping from the rising heat.

"We've got...about two minutes," Reggie said. "The heat will be almost two hundred degrees by then."

"Here, this is it," Gelp said, bathed in sweat. "I need some tape to fix the cut."

I still had the tape in my hand that we used to attach the table leg to the bat and gave it to Gelp. As he wound the tape around the wire, we heard more of the ceiling melt in globs. The temperature soared and Gelp was pouring perspiration.

"I...I can't see to finish," Gelp groaned as the sweat filled his eyes and he couldn't wipe it away.

So I took the tape and wound it as fast as I could, barely able to see through my own raining perspiration.

Suddenly, there was a series of popping sounds, a rush of electricity, and a gushing of cool air from the freezers. Everyone plunged inside his waiting appliance. Gelp literally jumped into a horizontal freezer, closing the lid like a coffin. I sprang to the freezer that was awaiting me.

The cold air inside the freezer was soothing. The metal doors had to be kept closed to keep the coolness in and it was an odd time of inner reflection. Actually, I pictured how weird it would've looked to anyone else to see us cramming ourselves into the freezers like we did.

Time passed very slowly. Little by little the freezer lost its coolness because of the heat pressing on the outside skin of the appliance. Or had the freezers turned off again!

We'd soon know. If they had stopped working we'd all be dead within a minute and the freezers would truly be coffins.

But even though the coolness was cancelled by the heat it never became bad enough as to be life-threatening.

Finally, there was a wrapping on my door. I opened it to see Reggie on the other side.

"Okay, it's over. You can come out, springer."

We were lucky that there wasn't any smoke because the fire was so thorough in its burning. It melted the roof material beneath it and caused it to evaporate rather than turn into smoke.

We all emerged from our freezers. The room was still very hot but not unbearablely.

Ty led us into the cafeteria where we found a large hole burned into the roof. The brilliant blue sky shined down on us.

"I guess that stuff of yours really works," Proof said to Reggie.

"You owe your life to it."

"Oh, yeah? Well, we wouldn't have got stuck down here in the first place if it wasn't for that material of yours."

"All right, stop the bickering," Ty ordered. "We've got other things to worry about. First – getting out of here."

A small mound of burnt ceiling lay beneath the hole. But it wasn't large enough to give a platform to stand on to be able to climb up through the roof.

Gelp and Ulfson solved that problem easily enough though by hefting one of the metal tables and lugging it to beneath the hole in the ceiling.

Ty pointed to me. "Springer, you go up first and do a quick scouting. Check for Emmonics."

"Right."

Just because I was younger than the others that didn't mean that I was spared dangerous missions if they were within my field of specialty. I was the lead scout for the team because of my uncommon agility and speed. Kivi helped. But in cases like this one, I went alone.

I decided to show off my abilities, particularly to Kivi. Instead of using the table to climb out I stood next to it and sprang out through the hole in the ceiling in one grand leap, finishing off with a well-timed summersault to the surface. A ten foot straight-up leap for me was easy. My limit was about thirty feet.

I heard bemused laughter and applause from below. I was especially glad to hear Kivi's.

It sounded even louder on the surface because here there was complete quiet. The pulsing silence was

hypnotic. There wasn't a wisp of a breeze at the moment –
which wasn't often - and the broiling white landscape
rippled in silent heat waves. The Emmonics had quickly
departed and there weren't any in sight.

I bounded across the area and carefully checked to
all directions to be certain I hadn't missed any signs of
movement. I hadn't. Then it was back to the hole in the
ceiling to give an all clear to the others.

The next one up from below was Kivi. When she
got onto the surface she immediately did a wider range
scouting of the area.

The others climbed out one by one and soon
everyone was on the surface.

Ty peered toward where our van had been parked.
"It's on its side," he reported. "Looks like the Emmonics
tore it apart pretty well." He started toward it. "Let's go
see what's left...if anything."

3

We walked toward the van in a group. When we got there we found it battered beyond any use. The Emmonics had attacked it as if it had been human, pounding it with boulders and the backs of their cleavers.

Gelp immediately went under the hood to check, but came up shaking his head.

"It's finished," he said. "They tore the electrical system out by the roots."

"Now what?" said Ulfson.

"We're going to need another vehicle," replied Ty, "which means we've got to find an old city or a place that might have one."

"There's an enclave about five miles north of here," Reggie said. "I was coming from there when the Emmonics ran me down."

"Okay, let's head there," Ty decided.

Gelp, Proof and Ulfson fished inside of the van to retrieve supplies from it that we needed. We were lucky that the food and water was still there, along with the baseball equipment like our gloves and baseballs.

Then it was northward. Ty gave me a nod which sent me and Kivi ahead to scout the terrain. I did the short distance scouting while Kivi would do the longer range recons because of her special abilities. On missions like this, Kivi and I would walk together for a while and talk before I sent her ahead.

For no reason in particular, we talked about the little people today. In this era, the little people were believed to be a new species of humans that were about the size of rabbits and were mutants created by the war. However, very few people had ever seen any of them.

"You spend as much time out here as I do," Kivi said, "have you ever seen any of the little people?"

"Yep, I got a quick glimpse of one of them once."

"Then you really do think they exist?"

"Sure."

"What do you think they are – like faeries or something else?"

"This is going to sound funny," I said, "but I think they're a cross between humans and crickets that developed after the war."

"Crickets! Why do you say that?"

"Because the one that I saw seemed to have a kind of back like a cricket might. The rest of him was human, but his back looked like a cricket's."

"I've heard stories about how the Emmonics are trying to wipe them out," Kivi said. "Why would they want to do that?"

"Ha, why do the Emmonics do anything? It's because of all of the burrowing and tunnel making that the little people do. It's a threat to the Emmonics' relics of the war – the debris and rubble."

Kivi turned to check behind us. We had already gone about a mile ahead of the others.

"Let's go on a little more before we separate," I told her.

"Okay."

I liked talking to Kivi and it was becoming harder and harder for me to let go of her during our scouting trips. She was becoming less and less like a sister; after all, we weren't in any way blood related.

"What about the living skeletons?" Kivi asked me.

"I haven't seen any of those yet," I said with great disappointment.

"Then you believe in them, though?"

"Sure. The idea makes sense."

"You mean that skeletons that had been thrown out of their graves by the bombs are roaming around the surface?"

"Right. The bones would have been irradiated by the bombs and once they'd been tossed onto the surface they would be given movement by interacting with the Earth's highly charged magnetic field. That seems very possible."

"Do you think they're alive, then?" Kivi asked.

"That's hard to say. These days, I wouldn't be surprised by anything."

"I think that's the only thing I'm afraid of," Kivi said, "running into one or a group of those skeletons."

"Just signal me if you ever do," I told her. "I'll be there before you know it."

I meant that in a special way, and for a moment our eyes touched in a special way. Kivi abruptly broke it off.

"I...uh, better be going ahead."

"Yeah, you're right," I replied. "Time for us to earn our keep."

With that, Kivi sped off forward for distant scouting.

The vastness of the land came around me. It was strange how the world was both widely open countryside yet somehow closed in and completely silent yet at the same time sprinkled with sounds.

I particularly liked the sound of the drifting fallout. That might sound odd, but by this time the fallout had lost most of its radioactivity and was totally harmless. It wasn't a common thing, but once in a while a person could feel a puff of wind flow past him and then hear a slight ringing sound as one of the transparent fallout clouds would sweep by and drop to the ground.

There was another effect I'd experience while alone in the wilderness, and it was the only thing that ever frightened me. Once in a while it would be as if some great curtain were raised and revealed a whole different world behind it and then the curtain would drop down again to cover it back up. I could see this other world for a matter of seconds before it disappeared again.

This could have been nothing more than a mirage. I doubted that though because it seemed like the same vision in the same way every time. A true mirage would be different every time.

It could also have been an insane delusion. But I doubted that too. What was truly scary was thinking that what I saw might be real. How could there be an entire other world right in front of us which couldn't be seen?

I was distracted from these thoughts by a signal from Kivi. She used the reflections from a small mirror to contact me and I could tell by the types and speed of flashes how seriously she needed me. Her current call was for me to come quickly, but that it wasn't a life threatening matter – just something important that I should see.

So, I sprang forward in a steady pace until I reached her. Kivi was squatting over a scattering of clothing.

"This hasn't been here long," Kivi told me.

"No, this isn't war debris for sure."

Kivi pointed forward. "There's more of it ahead."

"Let's go check."

Kivi and I very cautiously proceeded forward. Then we came to a sudden stop. A butchered body lay just behind a large boulder, the woman's head having been hacked off. We could see it in the near distance where it had rolled down a slight slope.

"Looks almost like she's been...sacrificed," I said.

"Whoever did it probably used the boulder as a type of makeshift altar."

"The Emmonics – a neat cut by a meat cleaver," I noted.

"Better warn Ty and the others."

"Right," I said. "I'll stand guard here while you go back and bring them. Make sure Ty keeps this spot under observation. I'll post myself on this boulder. If I should disappear for any reason that'll be a sign that there's still trouble here."

Kivi touched my hand lightly. "You better not disappear."

"Don't worry. I can out leap any Emmonic cleaver."

Kivi sped off to warn the others. I peered ahead toward a series of cliffs and ledges which housed the enclave that Reggie told us about. It was about a mile more distant but there weren't any signs of life.

This type of attack by the Emmonics wasn't common. It wasn't their policy to randomly slaughter people. While they were known to murder people who they thought were defiling their relics – war debris – they'd never been known to swarm and commit massacres. In fact, they generally travelled in only small bands.

I stood at my post until Kivi arrived with the others. We then marched in a group down the sloping dirt road that led to the collection of cave-side homes that made up this small enclave.

Despite his crooked right leg, Reggie lumbered ahead of us, dragging himself through the growing number of victims and debris. He'd known many of these people; they may have been his only friends on Earth.

The Emmonics had struck this place like a whirlwind. They whipped in and out of the hillside caves, dragging out their victims and insanely tossing whatever household possessions they came upon out into the open. Maybe it was a form of devotion to their god Blasteron. Who could tell?

We peeked into some of the cave-homes in search of survivors. The people here did not give up easily; there were many Emmonic dead among the victims.

This was very sad to see. It had been a thriving, well developed enclave as could be seen by the "modern" interiors of the homes. There were carpets on the floors and many of the hearths had been constructed out of remains of stoves and ovens. One home even had baseball cards – ancient ones – strewn on the floor.

Each of us separated on his own to search the area, but then we all eventually gathered at the community well which was in a large opening in the hills and under the sun.

"It's my fault," said Reggie. "If I hadn't just come from here..."

"You think they massacred these people just because the Emmonics knew you visited them?" asked Proof.

"I don't see why else they'd go on this rampage."

Ty then motioned for all of us to remain very still. "Maybe there's still somebody here who can tell us what happened and why."

"Did you spot somebody, Ty?" I asked.

He nodded. "Somebody just moved on the rim of the hill over my left shoulder."

"I can't see a thing there," said Proof.

Ty spoke to Kivi and me. "Springer, head to the right and make a circle to reach the top of the hill from behind. Kivi, go to the left and do the same. Start as if nothing's unusual. But when you get out of sight at the bottom of the hill, go into full speed. I think it's a survivor we're after, not a crazed Emmonic."

"Right," I said.

"You trap her from behind, we'll rush from the front."

"Okay."

Kivi and I left as instructed. In a very short time both of us had rounded the hilltop from behind and had come upon the person we were after. It was a young woman. She turned to run toward Kivi and me as the others rushed toward her from the front. Realising we had her trapped, she stopped dead in her tracks and...gave up.

The woman was dressed in white Emmonic robes which perfectly caressed her shapely body, especially as the light breeze wound the almost see through cloth around her. She had very long black hair and large green sultry eyes. I guessed her age to be about 25. She was too gentle looking to be an Emmonic.

Gelp forced himself in front of her. "You savages! Is that all you can do is kill!"

The woman answered in a shaky yet unafraid voice. "I'm not one of them."

"No, you just like to model their line of clothing," Gelp spat back.

"Hold on," said Ty just one moment before I would have spoken up. "I'll find out what's going on here."

"Well do it then!" shouted Reggie.

"Who are you?" he asked the woman.

"My name's Tina."

"An old world name," Proof noted.

He was right about that. Tina was a name common before the war and for me it brought up images of femininity, unlike the modern women. A woman named Tina would be the type who'd devote attention to her hair, her skin, her posture...and bathe a lot. Well, I was a...romantic.

"If you aren't an Emmonic," said Ty, "why are you dressed in their robes?"

"I was captured by them and taken by one of the men when my village was destroyed."

"There must be other Emmonics still around here then," Reggie said. "Are you the bait for a trap?"

"No, they've all left."

"And they just happened to forget you," remarked Gelp.

"The rest of them didn't care about me. When Ondroxx was killed...he was the man who captured me...during the attack on this place, that pretty much set me free. All I had to do was hide until they left."

"That makes perfect sense to me," I defended Tina.

But proof wasn't convinced, and asked, "If you aren't an Emmonic, then why did you run from us?"

"I didn't know who you were. You could've been crevice cannibals."

"We still could be, couldn't we?" Ty asked.

"No," Tina replied, flipping her long black hair to the right, letting the sun splash on her suddenly bare shoulder. "Crevice cannibals don't take the time to talk to their food."

"No, they don't," I agreed.

Tina's flimsy robe rippled around her as the breezes continued to swirl along the cliff.

"Wait a second," said Tina, pointing toward Reggie. "You're Trimagien, aren't you? The one they call the Blasphemer."

"Yes, I am the sinful one," he sarcastically responded.

"You're the cause of what's happening," Tina told him, pinning her fluttering skirts beside her.

"What does that mean?" Reggie asked.

"A holy war. That's why they attacked this village. That's why the Emmonics have vowed to keep attacking until they have you."

"Haven't we had enough wars for one planet," Ulfson commented.

"Yes, I found the last one to be quite enough," I spoke up, still trying to get Tina's attention.

"Well, the Emmonics are planning as big a one as they can," said Tina. "And since they outnumber the rest of us by about five to one our chances aren't that good."

"Maybe I should just surrender to them," Reggie snapped.

"Sounds like a good idea to me," Proof replied.

"And I'll leave the job of producing more of my atomic sheets to you," Reggie came back.

"All right, knock it off," Ty intervened. He then addressed Tina. "Do the Emmonics actually have some type of game plan their following?"

"There's a call for all of them to meet at their sacred shrine."

"I've heard rumours of such a place," said Ty. "Do you know where it's at?"

"No, not even most of the Emmonics seem to know where it's at either," Tina told him.

"Why do you say that?"

"Because people are going to have to be led there by what the Emmonics call 'Masters of Divine Hearing' who are special messengers who wear golden capes and carry magic staffs. At least, that's what I heard."

"Wow, I'd like to see one of those guys," I said, suddenly sounding much too childish to myself.

"Where do we come across them?" Proof asked.

"One of them is supposed to come to the village where I was being held prisoner," Tina told us.

"Okay," said Ty, "that's where we head. About how far away is it from here?"

"A day's walk at a normal pace," said Tina. "But there's the ruins of a good sized city about half way there where we can rest if we need."

"Maybe even find something there to drive?" Gelp asked as a question.

"Yeah, maybe," Tina told him.

"All right, let's head out," said Ty.

With that, we climbed over the rim of the hill and toward the vast, white, steaming plain below. For the time being, Kivi and I remained with the group instead of rushing ahead to scout the countryside. The land before us was pretty level and Ty's telescopic eyes would be able to spot any trouble immediately ahead.

I have to admit enjoying watching Tina from behind as she walked side by side with Ty. Kivi on the other hand seemed annoyed by my lack of response to her; I wasn't trying to be rude to her. But it had suddenly become very difficult for me to concentrate on other things because of our new addition.

4

We were closing in on the remains of what had been a small city. It had been well on the outer fringes of the nuclear strikes because some of its buildings were still standing. One of the structures was almost ten stories high.

I continued over to Ty and Tina who were still walking together.

"Ty, do you want us to go ahead and scout the city?"

Ty took a slow scan of the area, sweeping it for Emmonics, crevice cannibals or other clear dangers. He wouldn't send us into situations of obvious peril.

"Okay," said Ty. "Take a look around the edges of the place. Get a feel for it. But don't go directly into the city until we join up with you."

"Right." I motioned to Kivi, trying to impress Tina. "Let's go ahead."

She and I pressed forward in our usual way. Once we were clear of the others, Kivi let loose her anger.

"You sure are acting like an idiot all of a sudden," she whelped.

"What are you talking about?" Of course, I knew what she was talking about.

"Don't you think she's a little old for you?"

"You must mean Tina."

"Who else would I mean?"

"What did I do?"

"You danced all around her like a pribble cat."

"No I didn't."

"You were gaping at her so hard I thought a slark bird was going to fly into your mouth."

"I couldn't just ignore her. That would be rude."

"That would be rude? The over attention you gave her...that's rude!"

"You know, you may be right and that all may be true. But what do you care?"

Kivi's eyes were suddenly teary. "If you don't know, then I can't help you."

Kivi sprang off and was quickly out of talking range. And I felt like I had done something very wrong, but I wasn't sure what.

As I strode forward I noticed Kivi's movements in the foreground. For some reason, I now had a heightened sense of her.

The blasted out city loomed in the near distance. The few partially intact buildings were grouped together in the centre of town, looking like vultures grooming the countryside with their hungry gazes.

When I reached the edge of the city I tried to walk to where Kivi was but she kept a steady distance from me. It was very quiet on the city's border. The loudest sound was the wind rushing in and out of the open windows of the hollow buildings, sometimes causing a whistling sound as the remnants of drapes strained to escape.

The only other noise was the sound of objects in the insides of the building being tossed around by the winds in a never ending shifting of the interiors. There wasn't any sign of any living beings.

Finally, the others joined us.

"It looks pretty quiet," I told Ty.

Tina knitted her eyebrows. "I don't know," she said. "I hear something strange coming from one of the buildings."

"We discovered," Ty told me, "that Tina has super sensitive hearing to match my telescopic vision. Anyway, we should take her warnings seriously."

"What do you hear?" I asked.

"I'm not quite sure. It's not Emmonics or crevice cannibals. But it's like voices somewhere in the depths of one of the buildings."

"Like the little people?" Gelp asked.

"Yes! That might be it. Yes!"

"Maybe they're trying to direct us on, to finding a running vehicle of some sort," Gelp noted.

"What!" said Proof. He pointed into the distance toward the hopelessly crushed and damaged cars that were half buried in the streets. "From there."

"Of course not," Gelp told him. He motioned toward the tallest building. "See that. It was a hotel. It had underground parking and that's where we find a vehicle."

"Right," said Ty. "Great idea. But we're going to need some kind of light. We can't see in the dark."

"I got something to help with that," Reggie said. He withdrew a square, marble-sized object from his supply bag. "I call it a sunlight sphere. It's sunshine captured within a tiny magnetic field. When opened it time releases the photons over about an hour or two."

"Excellent!" said Ty. "Let's go find a vehicle."

We entered the blasted out town as a group. Stark-faced buildings lined both sides of the debris-heaped street, staring ahead in shock, wondering how they'd survived.

A slope of rubble was piled before the front double-doorway of the onetime hotel. Ty led us up the mound, through the shards of glass fringing the doors and into the dirt-heaped lobby. The lobby had suffered severe concussion damage as the chairs, desks, lamps, vases and other articles had been thrown into a furniture stew.

We marched through the debris – Kivi making sure to keep her distance from me – toward a side door that was marked STAIRS. Ulfson had possession of our lone baseball bat now and he had the honours of ramming the door open with it when it proved too hard to budge with a simple shove.

The smell of dirt and mildew and filth burst out. The darkness was as powerful. Reggie withdrew a simple flashlight for this, saving his sunlight sphere for later.

Tina froze us all with her warning. "S-h-h-h. I hear something."

Gelp then said, "And I saw something. Just out of sight. A little person scampered down the stairs."

Our over-excited catcher snatched the flashlight from Reggie and charged headlong down the stairs. We followed. As we did, I noticed tiny little footprints in the dirt.

Gelp slammed out the door at the bottom of the short stairwell and emerged in a spacious parking garage. When Reggie caught up, he broke open his sunlight sphere and tossed it into the middle of the garage, bathing the place in radiance.

The garage was half-filled with vehicles of all types and they were in excellent condition. Gelp was overwhelmed; he was in heaven!

"Great Pete Rose!" he exclaimed, "Look at all of these vehicles!"

"Take your pick," said Proof.

It didn't take Gelp long to single out a commercial-sized four-wheel drive vehicle.

"It would be nice if we had some extra gas we could take along with us," Proof observed.

That gave me an idea, remembering the generators that Reggie used in his former home. "These ancient hotels used to have emergency generators, didn't they?" I said. "They ran on gas, didn't they?"

"Yes! Yes!" Gelp shouted with glee. "And they'd be down here in the garage."

Ty patted me on the shoulder. "It was your idea, Springer, go hunt down a generator for us."

As I went on my search, I looked back to notice that Tina was smiling at me and nodding her head. She then called out, "Be on the lookout for little people...Springer. Don't scare them."

The sound of my name on her lips made me tingle. But at the same time I couldn't help notice Kivi glowering from behind one of the vehicles.

The light from Reggie's sphere spread to the very edges of the garage, but it wasn't nearly as bright there. Nevertheless, it wasn't hard to find the door marked – GENERATOR ROOM. But it was pretty dark inside and a flashlight would be needed.

"Found it," I shouted. "Bring a flashlight."

A couple of the guys came over and in no time we were carrying three large containers back to the four-wheel drive that Gelp was working on.

"Will it run?" I asked him.

"Sure it'll run. But the problem is getting it out of here."

We all flung a gaze toward the exit at once. It was covered by the upper outside wall which had caved in either during the bombing or from an earthquake. Either way, the exit was blocked.

"I think this is another chance for Reggie's atomic material to get us out of a hole," said Ty.

"Yes!" said Proof. "Burn away the debris."

And that's what we planned to do. While Gelp, Proof and Ulfson stayed behind in the garage getting the four-wheel drive loaded up and ready to leave, the rest of us went outside to the front of the building to work on removing the thick slab of concrete from the exit.

It was as Reggie removed one his sheets and lay it onto the slab that Tina made a frightening announcement. "I hear voices. And this time it isn't the little people, it's Emmonics."

"What!" said Ty. "Where?"

Tina pointed out past the boundaries of the town.

"I see them," Ty confirmed. "Looks like a hundred or more and coming fast.

"We've got another problem," Reggie noted. "We're going to need more than one sheet I think. That'll

48

take too much time if those Emmonics are coming at full speed."

"And they are," Ty told him.

"No!" cried Tina. "I don't want to be captured again! I'll kill myself first."

"We need a diversion," said Ty, using his managerial thinking. "And maybe separate them."

"Do you have a plan?" Kivi asked this time.

Ty pointed toward the distance – to the east and then the west. "Kivi, I want you to run off to the east as fast as you can, and Springer run off to the west as fast as you can. Make a wide circle and come to a meeting point in line with where we entered this city."

"I see," I said, "Some of the Emmonics will come after each of us."

"Right. And we should be able to handle the group that shows up here."

Reggie patted his bag. "Yeah, I got a few surprises in here to keep them back for a while."

"Just meet back up with us when we drive out of the city with our vehicle," said Ty.

"What if you don't come out?" Kivi asked.

"I guess you'll need a new team to work for."

"They're getting closer," Tina remarked.

49

I gave Kivi a friendly nod. She returned it, and the both of us sped off to the edge of the city in opposite directions. It was the two of us again working to help the team.

I never tired of loping through the open countryside, no matter the reason. The Emmonic horde caught sight of Kivi and me and did exactly what Ty expected them to do. They broke off into thirds; but one third was still heading straight toward the burned out city.

I later learned from Ty that things got pretty desperate as they waited for the second piece of material to burn a large enough hole through the concrete slab for the four-wheel drive to squeeze through.

The Emmonics were at the end of the block just as the last strands of material consumed themselves. Reggie then unleashed his surprise on the Emmonics – good old-fashioned dynamite. He and Ty tossed several sticks of the explosive at the charging madmen, tearing them to pieces, shredding their garments, throwing their cleavers to all directions.

Then the vehicle burst out of the underground garage. Reggie, Tina and Ty jumped aboard and the four-wheel drive roared down the street toward the remaining Emmonics. The robed maniacs were mowed down and cast to the side, squirming in the debris, venerating it as their last act.

Kivi and I joined up after making our long half circle each. The Emmonics chasing us were still far behind us, not nearly able to match our speed.

The four-wheel drive veered to the right and Kivi and I chased after it. It stopped only long enough for me to leap onto its roof and extend a hand down to Kivi who rode on the luggage rack up top with me. Gelp then howled with delight as the vehicle bucked forward and we easily outdistanced the Emmonics.

5

Since hearing of the Emmonic holy war and of the existence of their holy shrine our plans had changed. The goal now was to locate one of the Masters of Divine Hearing and have him lead us to this shrine. We would figure out what to do once we'd got there.

After escaping the latest Emmonic attack, we drove throughout the rest of the day without any other problems. It was actually quite pleasant. Kivi and I got very comfortable and sat side by side atop the four-wheel drive. We spoke very little – it would have been hard to speak over the background noises – and we wouldn't know what to say anyway.

I wasn't sure if she was still angry at me or not. I wasn't really sure of my feelings, either. But that still didn't keep us from enjoying each other's company. Both of us shared a love of the wide open spaces and we both found it particularly restful and soothing to be passengers atop the four-wheel drive and to have the luxury of gazing wistfully across the vast landscape.

This type of vehicle made us masters of the environment, which had many benefits. For one thing, it was much easier to hunt small game, especially the gopher-like animal which was called a diggler and was the staple of most travellers.

Digglers were the one great success story after the Mega War. They bred constantly. There were so many of them swarming in the wilderness areas that if you had a vehicle like ours all you had to do was drive around into a herd of them and snatch them up by their excessively long tails. It seemed that those tails were there for easy plucking.

That first night with our new vehicle we stuffed ourselves on roast digglers cooked over a fire started by using the internal cigarette lighter. Afterwards, Kivi and I strolled off together into the violet-darkened countryside while the others remained camped around the four-wheel drive.

A full moon floated over the tranquil landscape. The great orb's face always seemed to have a melancholy expression as if it were saddened by the ruined Earth it was gazing down upon.

"Our insane war even made the moon suffer," I noted as we strolled along.

"It's hard to believe that humans once walked on the moon."

"And we're now as far away from it as our cave man ancestors."

"I wonder," Kivi said, "if there were any humans on the Moon when...it...happened."

"Yeah, and were they stranded up there?"

"What kind of view did they have from up there of the world blowing itself up?"

There was a muffled explosion in the distance accompanied by what looked like a lightning flash. It was another previously undetonated hydrogen bomb exploding.

"There's been a lot more of those lately," I said.

"I hope no one was hurt by that one."

"Maybe we're having more earthquake activity these days to cause more bombs to go off."

As we both continued to peer skyward I saw one of my favourite sights. A tiny red dot of light passed slowly, elegantly through the stars.

"Look at that," I said with awe. "A satellite."

"There aren't many left anymore."

"The sky used to be filled with them before the war."

Satellites represented a special contact with the past, faithfully making their rounds through space, obediently following the paths they'd been assigned by masters no longer alive.

"I wonder what that world was like," Kivi said.

"It must've been a violent one," I replied. "Look what it led to."

"Or maybe it had just been an accident."

"One that the world couldn't afford to have."

Kivi and I returned to where the others were camped around the vehicle. I immediately noticed that Tina had removed her Emmonic robes and was now dressed in a loose fitting white blouse and a tight pair of jeans.

She, Ty, Proof and Reggie were gathered around the radio on the dashboard. It wasn't a typical car radio; it was much more elaborate and sophisticated, having a microphone attachment.

I crowded in with the others, pressing up lightly against Tina, who didn't seem to notice.

"What's going on I asked?"

"Listen," Tina told me.

I listened and heard a steady beeping sound coming over the radio's speakers. "What's it mean?" I asked.

"It means," Reggie replied, popping his purple head out, "that someone is trying to communicate with...someone."

"Maybe one of the Masters of Divine Hearing," said Tina, linking an arm around Ty's waist, getting a firmer position in the group.

"Or maybe a satellite calling home," I responded, withdrawing from the vehicle.

"What're you talking about?" asked Proof.

"Just what I said. A satellite just passed by overhead. Maybe it's still signalling Earth."

"Yes, that could be what we're hearing," Reggie noted. "Then again, it could be something else. We'll have to wait for more information."

A sudden rush of static across the radio washed away the beeping.

"Seems like a good time to turn in," Ty said. "We've got a big mission on our hands now and need to be clear thinking."

Our group around the radio broke up and each of us went off to find his own comfortable spot. I observed that Tina stayed with Ty and that Kivi had disappeared. So, I took a spot atop the four-wheel drive where I spent the night, rolling from side to side in my heated dreams.

Kivi had returned before morning and she and I were once again perched atop the vehicle as we continued cross country. Travelling had become a lot easier for a while because we picked up one of the former interstate highways which was still pretty much intact.

A constant horde of dust devils chased one another across the burning, dusty countryside. These miniature tornadoes were very common. Now and again we found ourselves having to either flee from them or stop in our tracks to let them go past. At least two of them twisted directly in front of us across the highway, giving us close up views.

We all kept our sight trained on the land in search of any of the Masters of Divine hearing that Tina told us about. They were our main target now and it turned out that locating one of them wasn't very difficult.

There was an intense glare of golden light on the eastern horizon. Gelp stopped the vehicle.

"Do you see that, Ty?" I called down, dangling over the side of the roof.

"Clear as anything. It's a man dressed in a flowing golden cape and carrying a long staff."

"That's one of them," Tina said. "Has he attracted a following, or is he alone?"

"All by himself," said Ty.

"Let's go introduce ourselves," Reggie said.

"Good idea," agreed Ty.

With that, Gelp diverted the vehicle from the highway and angled it at fast speed toward the man on the horizon. The four-wheel drive bucked wildly across the rugged ground and Kivi and I were tossed crazily from side to side atop the truck, desperately clinging to the luggage running rails along the rooftop.

Everything seemed to be rushing away from us. Dust devils flew by as if in terror of us. A pack of scaly scarp dogs went howling off in fright as we scared them from a diggler they were devouring. The oddest sight was a wandering piece of drapery that billowed over the top of the vehicle, almost clinging onto Kivi and me in its sweeping flight.

And then the brakes were hit and everyone lunged forward. Gelp stopped only a few yards from the man in the golden cape.

The Master of Divine Hearing defiantly stood his ground. He was a tall, burly man with stringy black hair which stuck out in places from beneath an old-fashioned airplane pilot's leather helmet with the nubs over the ears. His face was pig-like of appearance which was made the more grotesque by a pair of small tusks emerging from under his chin.

All of us dismounted and faced him, keeping a few feet back.

"I know who you are!" he grunted like a hog, his tiny pink eyes fixed fiercely on us. "The almighty Blasteron, our god of destruction, has delivered you into my hands."

Ty stood forward. "I think it's the other way around. You seem to be outnumbered."

The caped man put forward his long, smooth staff. "Not as long as I have this with which to direct the power of my god."

Ulfson then displayed his baseball bat. "This might not be as big, but I bet it'll pack the same wallop."

"I warn you to stay back!"

Then Ulfson did something foolish. He started toward the man, even though his intentions weren't really hostile.

"Listen," he said, "we just want to talk to you."

The caped man didn't want to talk. He shoved his staff forward and a powerful electrical jolt flashed toward

Ulfson, throwing him backward several feet. He hit the ground hard, his head cracking on a rock.

Both Kivi and Tina rushed to him. When they looked back up, their faces were grim.

"He...he's dead," Kivi said.

Proof picked up a huge stone and hurled it at the caped man. The rock exploded into fragments before it reached him.

"Damn you!" roared Gelp, rushing back to the vehicle.

He leapt inside, raced the engine, then roared at full speed toward the caped man. The caped man pointed his staff downward, touching the ground with it. A wide chasm was torn into the earth.

Gelp and the vehicle plunged into its depths. The rest of us were sucked downward into the sprawling, jagged crevice. Everything went dark for all of us.

6

Kivi and I were the first to crawl out alive from the crevice. Ty hauled Tina out and helped her revive on the surface. Then came Proof and Reggie who always carried the case with his atomic material near so he wouldn't be separated from it.

We sat together around the edge of the chasm, recovering.

"How long were we unconscious do you think?" I asked.

Proof gazed skyward, then answered, "Judging by where the sun is now, about 18 hours."

"Eighteen hours!" I cried. "We were in that hole all night?"

"Well, at least one night," said Proof.

"I wonder why the guy with the cape didn't finish us off," Ty questioned.

"Something must have scared him away," Reggie said.

"Him?" replied Tina. "He didn't seem like somebody who could be scared by anything."

"Nevertheless, he must've been," Reggie told her.

I don't know why I said what I said next, but I did. "I think it was the little people," I told them.

"Huh?" wondered Kivi.

"Sure, I kind of sensed them all around us. Maybe thousands of them. Too many for that caped guy to deal with."

"Springer may be right," Tina said, making me tingle again with the sound of my name on her lips. "I had the sense that they were all around, too."

"Well, whatever the reason we survived," Ty said, standing and peering across the desolate landscape. "We're sure stuck in the middle of nowhere now."

"So, what's next?" asked Proof.

"Let's head back toward the highway," Ty replied. "It'll be a lot easier walking down a paved surface. But first..."

Ty turned a full circle, looking over the area around us.

"Where's Ulfson?" I blurted out.

"He seems to be gone," Ty said.

"But...he didn't have a pulse when I checked him," Tina responded.

"I guess he got one back," noted Reggie.

"But where did he go?" Tina asked.

"Did he leave any footprints?" I sought.

"Good question," Ty said, scouring the ground around us.

The rest of us joined him. Ulfson hadn't left any footprints as far as any of us could tell.

"He was the only one who didn't fall into that hole," Reggie said. "Maybe..."

"Maybe?" Kivi asked.

"Cannibals."

"No, I don't think so," I said. "They would've left his bones. They never eat bones."

"Scarp dogs do," Proof noted.

"Then why didn't they eat us?" Tina asked.

"Because Ulfson wasn't eaten by anything," Ty spoke out. "He...wandered off somewhere."

"Dead?" I asked.

Ty joked, "He had a great attitude!" He then started forward, "Let's get moving before something attacks us."

We were all feeling pretty miserable as we trudged toward the highway which was about five miles away. The only food we had left were the nutrient pills that Reggie carried with him and our water supply was buried with Gelp and the four-wheel drive.

How things had changed in the last 24 hours! We were riding comfortably on a brand new all-terrain vehicle and dining on roast digglers. Now we were like marching zombies lost in the wilderness.

A conversation with a peculiar subject came up amongst all of us while we forged onward. It started concerning the man in the golden cape.

"Where do you suppose he gets his powers from?" Proof asked.

"It would seem to me," said Ty, "that it's somehow connected to that Emmonic shrine."

"How so?" asked Tina.

"Maybe the shrine is some type of storehouse of energy," Ty said.

"How could the Emmonics build something like that?" Kivi wondered.

"They probably couldn't," Reggie responded. "It's probably something left over from the old civilisation."

"Or maybe it was built for them by somebody," I broke in with a new thought.

"Built for them!" said Reggie. "Who? Why?"

"Aliens," I told him. "People from another planet."

"Okay," said Proof, "but why?"

"Because maybe the aliens want to use the Emmonics to destroy what's left of civilisation on Earth."

"Yeah," chimed in Kivi, "and maybe the man in the cape is really an alien. An alien sent to lead the Emmonics."

"You know, since the war, there have been a great deal of UFO sightings," Ty noted. "Maybe Springer has an idea there. Maybe we're really fighting aliens."

"You know, that somehow doesn't make me feel any better," Tina moaned.

Suddenly, the conversation shifted to something more immediate. Ty spotted a large object in the distance down the highway, but it was too far away for any of us to see.

Ty pointed in that direction. "There's something out there. And it's coming down the highway in our direction."

"Can you tell what it is?" Reggie asked.

"Some type of vehicle. The sun is glaring off its window. We've got to get to that highway to stop it right now."

"How far away is the vehicle?" I asked.

"Maybe twenty or thirty miles. But we're still pretty far from the highway, too."

"Then it's up to Kivi and me to get to the road and flag down whoever that is out there," I announced.

"That's right," said Ty. "But it might be dangerous. We haven't any idea who that is out there. They might be crazed killers for all we know."

Reggie reached into his case and pulled out a few sugar-cube-sized objects and handed some to Kivi and me.

"If there's any trouble, use these."

"What are they?" I asked.

"I call them knockout bombs," Reggie said. "You explode them at the feet of someone and they send off a cloud of vapour that will knock them unconscious."

"It'll knock us out, too, won't it?" asked Kivi.

Reggie withdrew a couple of other items from his case. They looked like ear plugs. "You won't be affected if you have these in your nostrils. They'll keep you from smelling the fumes."

We took the nose plugs and put them in our pockets along with the knockout bombs.

"All right, you two," Ty said. "It's up to you. Good luck."

We sprang off. This was one case where I had the advantage over Kivi. While it was true that she could sprint faster over a long distance she wouldn't be able to keep up her pace over a distance as far as this one. I, on the other hand, was adapted to longer distances at a slower speed. It would be like comparing a sprinter to a marathon runner.

So, instead of us separating this time, we actually kept up a steady jog with each other toward the highway. After a couple of miles, we were able to see the sunlight shining off the vehicle in the distance.

We finally made it to the highway, both of us panting and spent. But we had got there before the vehicle reached that spot. We stood right in the middle of the road and watched it approach; it was roaring down the highway at breakneck speed.

Kivi and I stepped off to different sides of the road to keep from being run down. We waved wildly as the vehicle neared at over a hundred miles an hour.

"They don't seem to be slowing down," Kivi noted.

"Ha, they're going so fast they might not even notice us."

"Or they think we're cannibals or Emmonics."

"I guess I better do something then."

What I did was plant myself directly in the middle of the highway.

"Springer! Get out of there!"

"I'll make sure they at least notice us."

I glared at the vehicle as it rushed at me. It was a medium-sized blue coloured laundry truck with the words KEN'S LAUNDRY written on the sides.   The only windows were the overly wide and high front windshield which was separated into two down the middle.

There was one man on either side of the window separator. They were both bald and crazy-looking - twins. I couldn't see if anyone was in the back of the truck.

The truck kept bearing down on me. I kept staring through the windows. The faces behind the glass got bigger and bigger. They saw me. Their eyes got so wide they reminded me of Hallowe'en jack-o-lanterns.

At the very last nanosecond I sprang straight upward. The truck ground to a stop, shuddering from the suddenness of the loss of movement. I dropped down to the surface about ten yards behind the truck.

The two men in the truck hung outside the open doorway on the driver's side as I approached from behind and Kivi came from the side of the road.

"What do you think you're doing?" the man who'd been behind the wheel asked.

"Getting your attention," I told him.

"Why?"

"We need a ride out of here."

"Where are you going?"

"Just out of here," I was noncommittal.

The other man then said in a dullish voice, "I don't think we're going that far."

"He's my brother, Tremb," said the driver. "He sees things differently than most people."

"This is my friend Kivi, and I'm Springer," I made our introductions.

"I'm Vapp."

"Yeah, Vapp's my brother," Tremb mumbled.

"You guys seemed to be in quite a hurry," Kivi said. "You nearly ran my friend down."

"It probably wasn't a good idea for him to stand in the middle of the road," Vapp replied.

"I got you to stop, didn't I?"

"Hey, Vapp," Tremb said in his slow voice, "We ain't got time to jabber here."

"Right. So why don't you two get in and we'll get going."

"We've got a bunch of friends who need a ride, too," Kivi told them.

"Where are they?" Tremb asked.

I pointed into the countryside. "They're heading toward us. We were sent ahead to stop you."

"You know, Vapp," Tremb said, "we are going to need all the help we can get."

Vapp peered worriedly down the road in the direction from which they'd just come. "Yeah, you're right, little brother." He then flicked me on the arm and told me, "I've got twelve more at home just like Tremb."

"Your mother must be...proud," Kivi said, winking at me as if at a joke.

"Okay, tell you what," Vapp said, "we'll detour from the road and pick up your friends. I think I can already see them coming toward us."

"Yeah, they're making quick time. One of our guys has telescopic eyesight and he probably saw that we've already stopped you and hurried everybody up."

70

"Telescopic sight!" said Vapp. "That will come in handy. Let's go." He motioned to the back of the truck. "You two get in back there - don't mind the crown."

Kivi and I hurried to the back of the truck, flung open the doors and climbed inside. The crown must have been the huge, pointed piece of metal that was propped against a wall. It looked something like a part of a woman's headband, but much too large for any normal-sized head.

We were soon bounding across the rugged ground and coming upon the rest of our haggard group. It wasn't long before we were helping Ty, Reggie, Proof and Tina into the back of the truck. I couldn't help notice how the perspiration pasted the front of Tina's blouse to her breasts. And Kivi couldn't help noticing where my attention had become glued.

Ty, Reggie and Proof crammed themselves toward the front of the truck so they could talk to Vapp and Tremb. Reggie was particularly interested in the extremely high-tech multiple band radio with which the truck was equipped.

"That thing looks like its powerful enough to contact the Moon," Reggie remarked about the radio. "But

I wouldn't think you'd have many people you could talk to with it these days."

"Not many," said Vapp.

"But we do hear a lot of things," added Tremb.

"Like what?" Reggie asked.

"Here, let me show you." Replied Vapp, turning on the radio and beginning to dial through the frequencies.

Suddenly, a sound broke through the static which was so astounding that it caused me to claw my way to the front of the vehicle.

"And here's the pitch," called the radio announcer. "And the swing. Oh boy, did he get ahold of that one. Way back, way back. No one's gonna get this. Hey! Hey! It's over the wall and onto Waveland Avenue, another home run for Ernie Banks."

"Ernie Banks," I said with reverence. "He played with the old Chicago Cubs during the 1950's and 60's."

Ty, Proof and I gaped at each other in dumbstruck amazement.

"It's not that hard to explain," said Reggie. "These are radio signals that have become trapped and have been circling the globe. No doubt the irradiated atmosphere keeps them from escaping into space."

"Yeah, but it's baseball! Real baseball from before the war!"

The broadcast continued for about five more minutes before being swept off the air by static.

"What a radio!" was Reggie's reaction. "Maybe this thing CAN contact the Moon."

He positioned himself at the base of the radio and began studying every aspect of it. Ty, Proof and I settled at the back of the truck, threw open the doors, and gazed out down the length of the road, dreaming of the bygone days of major league baseball.

A long parade of major league baseball players passed before me. Ty had amassed a huge collection of baseball cards that he'd taken mainly from partially destroyed sports stores and he would let me pour through it. I also started my own collection - based on Ty's methods - but I hadn't been as lucky as he.

My most prized possession was one of the yearly baseball encyclopaedias. These were massive books filled with statistics, biographies, and the box scores of baseball games. By reading the box scores a person could re-create much of the entire game in his mind, play-by-play as it happened. I spent many long hours doing that.

How odd it was that now we were peacefully riding in comfort in the back of a truck while just hours ago we were hopelessly lost in the wilderness. But that's what life was like after the war. We went from one crisis to the next with a period of tranquillity in between.

It was a desperate world we lived in. But at least there was a lot of freedom.

Then the next crisis struck!

7

Ty and I were still gazing at the highway which was retreating eternally backward behind us. I noticed that Ty's expression suddenly changed from one of dreamy tranquillity to one of utter terror.

He clawed the floor with his fingernails he was so horrified by what he saw.

"What's wrong, Ty?" I asked.

"I can only hope that what I'm seeing is a mirage or a delusion."

Tina came over and laid a hand on Ty's shoulder. "What's the matter?"

"There's something coming up behind us that I can't even describe. And they're going three times faster than this truck."

Everyone except Reggie, Vapp and Tremb joined us at the back of the vehicle.

"Duck!" Ty cried in panic.

Everyone flattened to the floor.

A tiny beam of blue light zipped over us and to the front of the truck. The ray sliced through the back of Tremb's head, killing him instantly. He fell out of the side door and we saw his body still rolling and bouncing on the asphalt of the road as we sped forward.

Vapp tried to speed up the vehicle but it wouldn't go any faster.

"Aren't you going to stop for your brother?" Tina shouted to Vapp.

"Why? He's dead, and I've got twelve more back home, remember?"

"What's out there chasing us, Vapp?" I asked.

"I don't know. Monsters of some type. They've been chasing us for the last fifty miles."

"I can see them now!" shrieked Tina.

"Yeah, me too," added Kivi, grasping my hand.

"Maybe they're aliens!" I cried.

We all could make out their shapes approaching down the highway. They were metallic dark blue machines with conical tops and skimming the ground in flight. Robots of some type!

"Vapp's right, they're some kind of mechanical monsters, Reggie," Ty told him as Reggie continued to fiddle through the radio controls.

"Which means they must have a weakness," responded Reggie.

As he said that, several new shafts of light stung through the truck, puncturing the walls. The force of the battering rocked the vehicle from side to side. Kivi and Tina were screaming.

The monsters came closer and closer. There was a squad of about twenty-five or thirty of them. They started to break ranks and were moving to surround us. Several of them flew past on the left and the right and eventually passed us.

Vapp ground the truck to a stop as a line of robots appeared before him. Those of us on the floor were dragged toward the front of the truck by inertia. The battering of light rays became overwhelming.

Then they suddenly stopped. The truck dropped dead on the road. The silence was pierced by a very high pitched whistling streaming from the radio. Tina crushed her palms over her ears against the noise which was especially painful to her extra-sensitive hearing.

We slowly unfolded from the floor. I climbed over the chair in which Tremb had been sitting and looked outside. All of the robots were frozen, now planted firmly on the ground.

"Ha!" said Reggie. "I knew it would work."

"What would work?" I asked him.

"I would be able to disable them if I found the right frequency."

"You're pretty smart, aren't you?" Vapp said more as an accusation as a compliment.

"More than smart," Reggie told him.

Vapp withdrew a luger from a compartment to his left and pointed it at Reggie.

"This is where you get out! I don't trust smart people."

"But you may..." Reggie started, but wasn't allowed to finish.

"Look, I don't care if you get out dead or alive."

Reggie picked up his case, then leapt out the front side door.

Vapp immediately floored the gas pedal and tore forward around the frozen robots, throwing us all back into a heap. He then closed the solid metal door that separated the front from the back and bolted it closed.

We were speeding so fast already that to jump out the back would have certainly caused serious injury. There was no way to help Reggie now anyway. His best hope was for us to stay with Vapp and eventually take control of the vehicle. But for now that didn't seem very likely.

We settled back and endured the ride. Tina fell into Ty's lap while Kivi and I sat side by side with arms linked. Proof seemed very annoyed with the way the four of us had paired up, and it wasn't because he was left out. He was a person who it was hard to get to know and he didn't seem to like it when other people chose to get along with one another.

The truck continued to race forward at a blistering speed. We spoke very little because it was very difficult being heard over the rattling noise of the vehicle's walls.

Finally, after about three hours, the truck began to slow down. And suddenly we were in another world, a world of such beauty that it could only have been a mirage! This was a place that could not exist in this world. But it did!

8

The sign read: WELCOME TO ROSELAWN - POPULATION 3,065. The laundry truck had turned down a road that led into a vast valley and we had entered the town of Roselawn. None of us were sure if we were hallucinating because such a place just could not exist.

There was one feature that convinced us of the reality of the place. The entrance to Roselawn was heavily guarded by the military, a very well-armed and regular military of mid-21st century vintage.

While a guard with a rifle questioned Vapp at the front door, a group of soldiers came around the back and peered in at us, rifles at the ready.

Vapp was ordered to unlock the door that separated us from him, and when he did we could hear the conversation he had with the guard.

"What's your citizen ID?" the sergeant asked Vapp.

"My ID is 45630vp00."

"What is your destination?"

"The Farnsworth Building," Vapp told him.

"And where have you been?"

"We were on a mission to retrieve our queen's crown. Our departure code was 6y789."

"Standby."

The sergeant walked to the nearby machine-gun-mounted jeep and checked a computer screen on the vehicle's dashboard. He came back a moment later.

"Only two people left at that time. Who are these others?"

"Lunatics I picked up along the way," Vapp replied.

"Escapees?"

"Probably."

"Well, you are going to the mental hospital. That's where we would've taken all of you anyway. Go ahead. But don't take any detours because you're going under close escort with orders to shoot."

"Sure. I just want to get home."

The sergeant stood back and waved Vapp forward. A couple of armoured vehicles followed closely.

I looked at the large piece of metal that was supposed to be part of a queen's crown and remarked, "If that's for their queen, she must be a giant."

"He called us lunatics?" muttered Proof.

"They all look crazy to me," I responded.

"Maybe so," said Ty, "but we're in their land now and they decide what's normal. Not us."

All of us moved as close to the end of the truck as possible to view the sight passing behind us. We had never seen anything like Roselawn before. It was a town that had been untouched by the war.

The streets were clean and paved and lined with houses that stood erect and bright in the sun. There were sidewalks, lush lawns, flower gardens and children playing in the yards. We even passed a baseball field with a manicured grass infield and stands for fans to sit in from which to watch the games!

"What a place for a baseball franchise!" I exclaimed.

"How could any place like this be?" Kivi wondered.

"It looks like not even radioactive fallout contaminated this place," said Ty.

We next passed a lake that was right in the middle of the town.

"I'll bet it's because of that water," Proof remarked. "Some type of continual updraft keeps recycling the air upward and pushing pollutants out."

"Makes sense," replied Ty.

The truck passed down several more streets before finally turning down a wide avenue that was lined with imposing limestone administrative buildings, glazed a warm yellowish-green by the sun. This road led directly to a long looping cul-de-sac street which had a huge five storey building at the point where it curved.

This great red coloured stone building was surrounded by a vast lawn which was protected by a tall, black wrought iron fence. Vapp steered the laundry truck in the visitor's parking space outside the building, then leapt from his seat and dashed toward the left side wing of the structure.

The army guards didn't try to stop him. Vapp joyously waved and shouted at a woman who was standing before one of the upper storey windows. She was dressed in flowing green robes and held a book in one hand and a flashlight in the other. Was this Vapp's queen?

A group of men dressed in white coats poured from the building and intercepted Vapp who willingly went with them. Another group of men in white descended upon our truck.

One by one we hopped out of the vehicle and were escorted up a long sidewalk toward the building. There was a group of people on the spacious lawn whacking large, wooden, coloured balls with mallets through a series of metal wire arch shaped hoops.

"What do you suppose they're doing?" Proof asked Ty.

"It sure isn't baseball they're playing."

"Yeah, but wouldn't that make a great baseball field," I exclaimed.

We climbed up a wide flight of marble stairs, passed through a couple of heavy oak doors and entered into a large reception area lighted by lamps that hung down from a very high ceiling. At this point, the army guards that had been following us departed, leaving us in the hands of the security people here.

Our little group was led into a fancy, private office to the right. It took the breath out of me it was such an elegant room. The many chairs were heavy and thickly stuffed and covered with a shiny type of material. Huge wooden bookcases loomed from the walls, a great globe of the world took up a place in the corner in a tripod cradle, and a massive desk of oak sat defiantly before a pair of opened windows which looked out onto a rose garden.

A middle-aged man with a full head of black hair and who was dressed in a neat blue suit sat behind the desk. He motioned for us all to take our seats while a group of burly men in white cordoned off the back of the room. They had taken the place of the security team. These men weren't only hulking but they were armed with chains, handcuffs and billy clubs. It was clear that we were now prisoners.

"I'm Doctor Kreider," the man behind the desk introduced himself. "You've been brought here for observation."

"Quite a place you have here," Ty said. "It would make a nice home for the new Hall of Fame."

"It's pretty rare for us to get visitors here in Roselawn," the doctor said, "and when we do we like to run a thorough check on them - make sure no unwanted manias or hysterias are unleashed."

"Oh, is there a type of preferred mania or hysteria that you would like to unleash here?" Proof joked.

"I assure you, young man, this is a very serious matter."

"I'm sure."

"How do you account for the existence of a place like Roselawn?" Ty questioned.

"What do you mean, account for?" Kreider asked.

"Well, the rest of the world is in ruins. This place looks like it hasn't been touched at all by the war."

"Well, World War Two was a very long time ago. And we weren't really affected by it on this continent."

"No, I'm talking about the last war," Ty said, confused. "The nuclear war."

"You actually believe that there was a nuclear war?"

"We've seen plenty of evidence of it all across the country."

"I'm very sorry to hear that."

"Yes," said Proof, "the nuclear war was a great inconvenience to a lot of people."

"I see, young man, that you are going to require special attention. Heavy sedation, probably."

"Wait a minute," said Ty to Kreider, "are you trying to say that the nuclear war never happened?"

"Of course it never happened. It's a mass delusion that plagues a certain portion of the population. Fortunately, most of these people can be cured."

"Cured of what?" I asked.

"Young people like yourself respond particularly well to treatment," he told me.

"Treatment for what?"

Standing, Kreider placed his hands on his hips and scanned us. "Let me ask you this: when did this supposed nuclear war happen?"

"About 220 years ago," Ty told him.

"Were you there at the time?"

"Do I look like I'm 220 years old?"

"Then you don't have actual first-hand knowledge of this presumed war," Kreider noted. "Do any of you happen to know anyone who was there when the war happened?"

"Of course not," said Ty.

"Then where did you get your information about the occurrence of this nuclear war?"

"Word of mouth," Ty replied with disgust.

"Isn't it more likely," said Kreider, "that you made up this story about the war to explain away your own guilt and inadequacies?"

"You make less sense than a brick in a road," Proof responded.

Kreider became enraged! "How dare you address me like that?"

"I don't know how else to address a madman!" returned Proof.

Kreider motioned to his gang of white-coated guards. "Enough of this! Take them all back to rooms 2b and 2c for immediate treatment."

The gorilla-sized guards pounced on the others and easily overpowered them. But when a couple of them reached for me I was able to elude them by springing straight upward.

They weren't expecting that. When I came down I landed atop Kreider's desk and used it as a springboard to fly out his opened windows.

"Let him go for now," were the last words I heard Kreider speak, "we'll get him later."

Expecting that a search party was already being sent out to track me down, I located a patch of tall shrubbery near the building I'd just fled. I chose to hide there instead of trying to flee. No one would look for me only a few feet outside of Kreider's office - I hoped.

I listened closely to all of the sounds around me. A search party was sent out, but it was sent out in a direction away from where I was hiding. When all of the noises around me died down and it seemed quiet inside Kreider's office, I decided to move.

I hurried the short distance back toward the doctor's office. Peeking through the window, I saw that the room was empty and the door to it had been closed. So I climbed back inside through the window, thinking that this would be the last place they would look for me. My plan then became to wait until dark and, when most of the staff was gone, try to find the others and help them escape.

It would've been foolish to try to do that now. The halls were patrolled by white-coated guards and the building was busy with activity.

So, I waited.

Screams of pain and anguish echoed down the corridors and severed the silence of Kreider's office. Was one of those shrieks made by Kivi? Tina? Even Ty or Proof? No, I could tell it wasn't any of them. If it had, I couldn't have stayed inactive. I could only imagine the tortures that went on in this place in the name of therapy.

I had to force myself not to charge into action too soon. What good would it do anyone if I was overpowered? Desperate for distraction, I grabbed a book from one of the shelves and skimmed through it.

By sheer chance the book that I took was a military history of World War Two. It was filled with photographs of destroyed cities and the weapons that had been used to destroy them.

The devastation of Dresden in Germany was particularly shocking, but it was the leftovers of Hiroshima and Nagasaki that struck me hardest. They'd done it once before and hadn't learned from it! They had to do it on a worldwide scale!

The sun was beginning to set. The faded red light filtered through the office windows which faced to the west. I sat in a corner of the room out of sight with the book open in my lap and was bothered by a bizarre thought.

What if Doctor Kreider was right and the nuclear war was some type of mass delusion? What made me think of this was remembering those times when I was alone in the wilderness and I had brief glimpses of another world in existence at the same time as ours. Were we the ones who were insane? Or was it just me? Is it possible that Kivi could see this mirage world at times, too? I wondered.

9

The hallways had become quiet. An occasional cry of pain still pierced the air, however.

Someone was coming down the hall in my direction. I could hear the footsteps echoing louder and louder. I pulled back as far against the wall as I could. Even though I couldn't see the door, I could feel a face press up against the glass window and peer inside.

A hand grabbed the doorknob and I dug my fingers into my pocket. I grasped my nose plugs and one of the knockout bombs I was still carrying.

A long, drawn out scream erupted from somewhere down the corridor and whoever was about to enter Kreider's office changed his plans and he ran to the direction from which he'd just come. At the same time, there was a series of loud pounding sounds from outside which I assumed was from a thunderstorm.

It was time for me to leave my hiding place and to save my friends. I went to the door, saw that the hallway was empty and I squeezed out through the narrow opening I spread apart for myself. Leaping to the wall I inserted the nose plugs in my nostrils, inching my way along, gazing into the rooms as I passed them in search of the others.

Room after room went by. Some of them were empty. Some were typical hospital rooms with patients in their beds. One room was used for shock therapy which I could tell by the furnishings.

And then, I found Ty and Proof. They were both bound in straitjackets in the same padded cell and were leaning back against opposite walls. I tried the door, but it was locked. They both heard the noise and looked expectantly up at me.

I turned from the door to find something with which to break in. Then a pair of thick, monster arms grabbed me around the waist from behind. Instead of struggling, I fell absolutely limp. My attacker was so surprised that he let go of me. As I oozed downward, I withdrew one of the knockout bombs and threw it to the tiled floor.

The pellet shattered and let loose a thick cloud of gas which instantly knocked out the white-coated guard. He carried a chain of keys on his belt which I grabbed. I found the right key and went into the padded cell where I helped Ty struggle out of the straitjacket. Then we each released Proof.

"Kivi? Tina?" I asked. "Where are they?"

Both men shook their heads, groggy from sedation and apparent physical abuse. I helped both of them into the hall and their strength and agility slowly returned as we sneaked around the first floor of the building.

We crisscrossed the corridor, bounding from room to room in search of Kivi and Tina. Ty located them at the far end of side hallway which dead-ended. Proof and I rush to the room and I found the key on the guard's chain that opened it.

Both Kivi and Tina were strapped into their beds. Tina immediately responded when we hovered over her and we started undoing the thick leather straps. Kivi remained totally motionless.

"They did something to her," Tina told us. "Some type of electrical shock therapy."

"Damn it!" I gritted my teeth. "If I'd known I could've tried to help her."

Ty patted me on the back. "We can only do the best we can, Spring." Spring was his seldom used big brotherly term of affection for me.

"That's right," Proof added, "You wouldn't have had a chance against this army of guards they have here."

"Let's get Kivi onto a gurney and wheel here out of here," Ty instructed.

"To where?" asked Tina.

"The laundry truck!" I blurted.

"Right," said Ty. "If it's still there. Let's get Kivi and go."

We did as Ty instructed and I helped lift Kivi onto the gurney. She was still alive, but completely oblivious. I couldn't bear to see her like that and then I realised my true feelings for her.

The five of us went into the hall and started forward. Suddenly, a group of guards appeared at the end of the corridor. They were so massive of build that the four men blocked the entire exit.

We froze. We couldn't turn around because it was a dead- end. The guards remained motionless where they were, blocking our only route.

Reaching into my pocket again, I pulled out a couple more knockout bombs and hurled them at the feet of the guards. The result was the same as before. They dropped like stones, unconscious. The fumes were far enough away so as not to affect us, and we started forward again.

But just as we wheeled Kivi around the unconscious guards and headed toward the front door, Dr. Kreider appeared before us with another group of guards. And they were all wearing surgical masks to protect them from the fumes of the knock out bombs.

"This is as far as you go," boomed Kreider.

More guards arrived behind us. We were completely trapped.

"Let's go out fighting!" I declared. "Make them kill us before we ever give in."

"What about Kivi?" asked Ty.

I had no answer.

Kreider waved to both sets of guards and they started marching toward us, billy clubs raised. We posed for battle.

But it was to be postponed. A mighty explosion slammed the walls. The entire building rocked to the foundations. It actually seemed to sway.

The force of the explosion was so powerful that Kivi was partially shaken off the gurney. The rest of us were either shoved to the floor or into the walls.

It was amidst dead silence that we all slowly rose to our feet.

Then coming through the front door was the most welcome sight I had ever seen! Reggie! Accompanied by one of the robots that had attacked the laundry truck.

Kreider and the three guards with him stormed toward them.

"Cylix one," Reggie ordered the robot, "apply a heavy stun force to the four nearest individuals approaching us."

With that, a wide red ray was dispersed by the robot toward Kreider and his men, felling them instantly. The other guards fled in mad panic.

We rushed toward Reggie, crying his name aloud with exultation.

"I never thought I'd say this," said a tearful Proof, "but am I glad to see you!"

"Naturally," said Reggie completely in character. "So, what's been going on here?"

"This is an insane asylum," Ty told him. "The doctor was trying to convince us we were all crazy."

"And then try to cure us," added Tina.

"What about Kivi?" Reggie asked.

"They did something to her," I excitedly answered. "Some type of shock therapy."

"That isn't good," remarked Reggie. "The effects could be permanent."

"You mean..." I said.

"She may never come out of it."

"And it's my fault."

"Your fault?" Reggie responded. "How is that?"

Ty answered for me. "He doesn't think he acted quick enough to try to help us escape."

"Oh," was the only reply.

I walked closer to Kivi and stared down into her motionless, dreamless face. "We've got to help her."

"Now that we seem to have control here," Ty said, "let's get her back into one of the rooms and keep watch over her until morning."

"That's a good idea," agreed Tina. "Maybe when Kreider wakes up he'll be able to tell us how to help her."

"I think we could all use a good night's rest," said Proof. "I'm still a little groggy from their drugs."

"Do you want me to put the straitjacket back on you?" Ty joked.

"No, the sleeves were too long."

"Okay," spoke Reggie. "Let's get some good rest tonight and finish our job here tomorrow."

"What do you mean?" Ty asked.

"This town is a satellite tracking centre," Reggie told us. "We might be able to control from here some of the satellites that are still in orbit."

"If we could do that we could almost rule the world," I noted.

"Almost?" said Reggie.

"What about these robots?" asked Proof. "Are they yours now?"

"It was just a matter of re-programming them. And, yes, they'll follow my instructions now."

"I see you still have your case with the atomic sheets," Ty said. "Don't you think that these robots could burn away the debris better than the sheets?"

"No, the sheets will still be more efficient. It would take the robots hours to burn away the same amount of debris that the sheets could do in minutes. And the sheets won't leave a trace."

Ty walked down the hall a short distance and looked outside. "How safe are we?" he questioned Reggie.

"I've already given their military a lesson in my superiority," was the response.

"Then that must've been the explosions I heard earlier," I observed. "It wasn't a thunderstorm."

"Right. I had my robots blow up a couple of their tanks when they refused to get out of the way."

"Just blew them up, huh?" said Proof.

"No point in arguing. In fact, I'm going to go outside and place the robots on guard around the building so that we're completely protected."

"Need any help?" Ty asked.

"Hardly," Reggie scoffed and then left the building to deploy his robots.

"I hope that someone doesn't go mad with power," Proof remarked.

"Well, this is a madhouse," I joked.

We found rooms for the night and let Reggie's robots - which had the power to levitate objects - deal with putting Kreider and his men in confinement.

Ty and Tina roomed together. Proof settled in Kreider's office. Reggie disappeared somewhere in the building. And I stayed with Kivi in the original room from which we moved her.

What if Kivi never recovered? It was only with her possible loss that I realised how important she really was to me. Who else shared my love of the open countryside as she? Who else could keep up with my pace and make long distance journeys through barren wilderness fun? How lonely it had been before I met her. How lonely it would be if I lost her.

With those thoughts percolating through my brain, I finally dropped down onto one of the beds and fell into a fitful sleep.

I was awakened the next morning by the sound of the hospital staff performing its daily routine. It was as if nothing had changed for them. None of them seemed to care about the different people who were now in control of the building.

Ty and Tina came into the room to check on Kivi.

"No change," I told them. "She's the same as she was last night."

"I wish I knew what to do," Ty said, shaking his head. "But I will come up with something. It's just a matter of time. A little more time and I will think of something!"

"You know," I responded, "that's one thing that we do seem to have plenty of right now - time."

"What do you mean?" Tina asked.

"Are we really in such a rush to leave this place?"

"You do have a point," Ty replied. "Now that Reggie's robots have this place under control for us, there doesn't seem to be any hurry to leave."

"Are you both forgetting the Emmonics?" asked Tina. "They're massing for a final holy war."

"I'm not talking about staying here indefinitely," Ty replied. "Just a couple of days, or weeks even. Maybe that'll be enough time for Kivi to recover."

Reggie abruptly entered. "Okay, everybody - break it up. We've got work to do."

"What work?" asked Ty.

"Remember: we've got to get to the satellite tracking centre."

"That's right."

"Not before we get some real food to eat," I told him.

"He's right," Ty agreed. "How long has it been since we've eaten anything?"

"Way too long," said Tina.

"Okay," said Reggie, "this place has a pretty nice cafeteria. It kind of reminds me of my old place - the same type of green tile. I could use something to eat, too."

We left a robot on guard over Kivi and then the rest of us, including Proof, had a full breakfast. None of the cafeteria servers cared who we were or seemed to have noticed that anything was out of the ordinary. They were happy, however, with the large tip we left them. Reggie had taken the money from the cash register the night before.

After breakfast, Reggie led Proof, Ty and me out front to the army jeep that would be our transportation. Tina decided she'd rather stay behind and rest and look in on Kivi.

We drove away from the asylum without anybody bothering us; nobody cared. I wondered if we really even needed our escort of six robots.

"Reggie, did you ever find out where these robots came from?" Ty asked from behind the steering wheel. "Are they some kind of alien army?"

"No, they're an obscene leftover from the nuclear war."

"What isn't?" remarked Proof.

"These robots are a doomsday squad created by a secret military agency to kill any and all survivors of the nuclear war."

"You mean they've been roaming around for the past 200 years killing things?" I asked.

"No. They had been trapped in an underground vault until one of those undetonated nuclear warheads went off near their position and released them."

"Ha, the war that keeps on giving," said Proof.

"No matter who built those robots or why," Reggie said, "they'll sure be a big help in our war with the Emmonics."

"If the robots don't run out of power and die on us," I noted.

"Not much chance of that," Reggie told me. "They're all powered by a radioactive isotope with a half-life of 10 million years."

"Which means what?" I questioned.

"They'll still be running fine 10 million years from now."

"That should give us enough time to defeat the Emmonics," Proof said.

"How smart are these robots?" Ty asked.

Reggie snorted. "Smart? They're actually pretty stupid. They have to be precisely programmed before they can do anything."

"There's one thing that really worries me about them," proof said. "What if someone else gets control of them like you did, Reggie?"

"That's not likely to happen," replied Reggie. "And once we get control of those satellites we'll have control of the world and nobody will be able to stand against us."

"Is that really such a good thing," I remarked.

"What's that mean!" wondered Reggie.

"Some time too much power can cause too much trouble for the person who has it," Ty told him.

"That's a philosophy I don't accept," stated Reggie.

It became very quiet in our jeep as we headed into the business section of Roselawn. We had only seen the residential part of the city so far and this section of town was eye-opening in its modern features.

There were many instances of preserved technology. Roselawn had two local television stations, three radio stations, sodium-vapour street lights, microwave towers and a nuclear power station that supplied energy to the town.

As impressive as all of these was the satellite tracking complex on the edge of Roselawn. It was located in a three storey blockhouse like structure that was surrounded by a variety of fan-shaped radio signal receiving dishes.

The inside of the building looked a lot like the pictures I had seen of NASA's central command in Houston which had long since been pulverised.

A corps of technicians sat behind rows of computer consoles, monitoring numerous satellites that were still orbiting the planet. They either weren't aware of our sudden arrival in Roselawn or didn't care, going about routine as usual. They didn't seem bothered by the robot that accompanied us, either.

The locations of all of the satellites were displayed as tiny blinking lights upon a vast screen that took up one entire wall.

Reggie stood behind one of the technicians and asked, "Are any of these satellites still operational? Just because they're still in orbit doesn't mean they're functioning."

"Still operational!" barked the technician. "Of course they're operational. Do you think we'd sit around here monitoring a bunch of useless space junk?"

"Okay, then how many of them are armed? Satellites with nuclear capabilities were used during the last war."

"Are you kidding, Mack! They didn't have more than a couple atom bombs during World War Two."

"I was referring to the last war," said Reggie.

"Me, too. I don't know of any other."

It then occurred to me that Reggie probably didn't know that the people of Roselawn were in denial of the nuclear war. It must have occurred to Ty at the same time because he told Reggie, "The people in this town don't believe there was a nuclear war."

"Well, judging by this place, it doesn't look like they had one here."

"Sure," I said, "maybe it's the last place left on Earth to settle down and raise a family."

"Until the Emmonics interrupt things," growled Reggie.

"I wonder why they haven't yet," said Ty.

"I plan to make sure they don't have the chance," announced Reggie. "First, let's see if we can target something with one of these satellites."

He then told the technician, "Lock onto one of the military satellites."

"I can't do that without permission from my supervisor."

"Don't worry about him. I'm taking over."

"Ha! On whose authority?"

Reggie pointed toward the robot. "His."

"I don't recognise his authority."

"I'll fix that."

Reggie then addressed the robot. "Cylix three: administer a level 5 dose of pain to the being directly in front of you for a duration of 46 seconds."

A beam of yellow light engulfed the technician who stiffened in his chair in extreme pain. All of the other technicians were watching, many of them striking to their feet. When the 46 seconds were up, the light was extinguished and the man fell back into his chair with great relief.

"All right, all of you!" Reggie called out. "I am now in control of this complex. It will be useless to argue any of my commands."

Everyone seemed to understand; and those technicians who had been standing resumed their seats.

"Pretty effective," Ty noted.

"Almost even tyrannical," Proof added.

"We haven't time for etiquette," Reggie replied. "We have an enemy who are a lot more ruthless."

"He's right," I agreed. I was also remembering our initial vicious treatment in this town. "But let's remember not to be as bad as the enemy or there's no difference."

"Wait a minute," said Ty. "Maybe if I add a little something to what you told these people, Reggie, we can get their voluntary co-operation."

"Go ahead."

"Listen everyone, there's a reason we're doing this. What none of you know is that Roselawn is about to be surprise attacked by an army ten times the size of yours. We're trying to stop them to protect you."

The effect of what Ty told them was visible. They didn't quite hate us as much.

"All right," said Reggie. "Now let's get those satellites working for us."

Reggie once again addressed the same technician. "Lock onto one of the armed satellites."

With minor hesitation, the technician did as he was instructed.

"Okay, now we need to lock onto a target, something of no importance."

"How about the landfill?" the technician suggested.

"Perfect," said Reggie. "Can one of the satellites bring up a visual image of the landfill on the screen?"

A moment later, just such an image came up.

"Good," said Reggie. "Fire whatever weaponry the satellite is equipped with at the landfill."

This was done. A blast of concentrated laser struck the landfill and tore a section out of it."

We were shocked by the cheer that went up.

"Well, these people have a real fighting spirit," Proof remarked.

"Good, because they may have a real fight ahead of them with the Emmonics," I replied.

"Now all we have to do is locate the Emmonic shrine," Ty said.

"We should be able to do that in a few minutes," Reggie responded.

"What!" Proof cried.

"That shrine has to be emitting a great deal of energy. We should be able to pinpoint it by using one of the tracking satellites."

"Well let's do it then," said Proof.

Reggie took a seat at one of the consoles. After a quick scan of the controls, he began to operate them. He donned a pair of earphones and listened closely to signals being picked up by one of the antennas.

"That must be it," he reported. "An extremely powerful electro-magnetic emission from a point about 350 miles north northwest of here." He worked a few more of the controls. "There, on the screen - the green, blinking light."

"That's near where Joliet, Montana used to be," I noted.

"And I'll bet that's where the Emmonic shrine is," Reggie told us.

"Can't we just vaporise it from here?" Proof asked.

"No. We'd need a lot more precise co-ordinates. We'll have to have someone on the scene to relay them back here. It's not the same as firing on a landfill in your own backyard. And, we can't be absolutely certain that the emissions are coming from the shrine. And ...maybe we don't want to destroy it."

"What!" said Proof.

"Who knows what type of scientific marvel it might really be?" replied Reggie. "We have to at least see it up close."

"Right," said Ty.

"No matter what we do," I said, "I think we're going to have to have one of us here operating these consoles."

"Yes. My robots won't be able to do that. Someone will have to stay behind."

"Who?" I asked.

"Tina seems the most likely," Ty said.

"Why?" questioned Reggie.

"She may have to stay with Kivi to look after her."

"No!" I cried. "Kivi goes with us. She's my partner."

"Not in the condition she's in, she isn't," said Proof.

"Listen! Kivi goes with us!"

"Hold on a minute, Springer," said Ty. He then turned to Reggie. "You seem to know a lot more about Kivi's condition than the rest of us."

"Yes, I've studied catatonic states."

"Tell me, then, is she more or less likely to break out of it as time goes by?"

"Much less likely. She actually drops deeper into oblivion with each passing day."

That actually hurt me to hear that.

"Here's what we'll do then," Ty stated. "We'll train Tina how to operate the computer consoles here and leave her behind, regardless of Kivi's condition. And tomorrow we'll either bring Kivi out of her coma or not. If we do, she comes with us. If we don't, she stays. One way or another, we leave tomorrow!"

Ty asserted his leadership in a way he hadn't done for a while. And no one argued with him.

111

10

There had not been any improvement in Kivi by the next morning. Our vehicles had been loaded with provisions, Tina had been shown how to operate the computers in the satellite control centre and she would be given command of a number of the robots to assure her safety when she officially took over.

And it was time to deal with Kivi. She still lay motionless in her bed; worse than before. Ty had a plan to try to rouse her from her deadened state of mind but hadn't told any of us what it was. It had to be something desperate, we all knew that.

Proof, Reggie, Tina and myself could only watch and wonder what he possibly could do to help her. There were also three burly custodians on hand - working for us now - to assist, but they hadn't yet moved.

Ty walked over to the case in which Reggie kept his atomic sheets. We couldn't figure out what he was doing when he lifted the lid and took one of the sheets out.

Without a word, Ty whipped the sheet in the air to unfold it and then carried it toward Kivi. My mind exploded with horror. He was going to lay it on her. Why!

Yelling with insane abandon I flung myself toward Ty to try to stop him.

"No! No! I won't let you kill her like that!"

Reggie and Proof pounced upon me but I fought loose. Then the three custodians fell upon me and forced me to the floor, shouting and squirming.

Ty lay the sheet upon Kivi. At first there was no response. Then, all of a sudden, she jerked forward as if she'd been shoved from behind. Her eyes burst open. She shrieked and clawed at the sheet that was on top of her. Ty quickly yanked it away.

Then it was over. Kivi sat up normally and peered around the room, fully conscious.

The custodians released me and I sprang to my feet. I slowly walked over to Kivi who stretched out a tiny hand to me. As we touched hands, we shared each other's gaze of wonderment.

The others gathered around us.

"That was brilliant, Ty," Proof said to him. "You did a great job."

"Don't congratulate me. Springer did most of it."

"What!" I cried.

"Sure, it was more your reaction than anything else that got Kivi's response and made it all real for her."

"I still don't understand," I said.

"Well, Kivi knew what the atomic sheet could do, but this one hadn't been activated so she couldn't really have a physical response to it. But she saw your response which convinced her that the sheet really was about to incinerate her."

"Why didn't it?" Tina asked? "Why didn't the sheet start burning?"

"According to Reggie," Ty said, "the sheets are activated by the radiation in the atmosphere. There isn't any radiation in Roselawn's air, probably the only place in the world like it."

"Ty, that was brilliant!" Reggie told him. Reggie! "You knew that subconsciously she was alert to everything."

"Let's see what Kivi's got to say," Ty responded.

"You never stop amazing me, Ty," Kivi responded. "But I sure want to get out of this place as soon as possible!"

That brought a subdued cheer from the rest of us.

Ty motioned to one of the staff who was in the hall with a breakfast cart. She wheeled it into the room.

"Before Kivi goes any place," Ty said, "she'll need something to eat."

"I'm starving!" replied Kivi.

It wasn't long before the six of us were in the two armoured jeeps and heading toward the satellite tracking centre followed by a guard of eighteen robots.

When we arrived, Tina was installed in command of the operations there. She was now given direct command of four of the robots. It was made clear to the staff, that if for some reason Tina were threatened in any way Reggie would destroy everything in the town of Roselawn. Everything!

Then we left. Ty and Reggie were in the lead jeep, and Kivi, Proof and I were in the second one. The reason we didn't take the larger armed vehicles was because they would need too much fuel, and the smaller vehicles would be easier to manoeuvre. Beside, we had all of the firepower we needed in our squad of robots. Anyone could control the robots when using a microphone that Reggie had specially designed for that purpose.

It was difficult leaving Roselawn, a preserved memento of the past when life was "normal." But it would certainly be a nice place to return to when this last war was over.

Roselawn was located in the southwest corner of what used to be Kansas. The highways in this part of the country were in pretty good shape because not too many of the bombs were lobbed into what was farm country.

There was a lot less debris here, too. But that meant that all of the open farmland was contaminated by heavy radioactive fallout and would be useless for agriculture for hundreds of years. The only useable land was buried under the protection of tons of debris. That's why Reggie's material was so vital to getting civilisation growing again.

Of course people had tried to remove the debris with explosives but what that did was spread the fallout from the top of the debris into the air and then onto the ground which was then made useless.

"We're picking up movement ahead," the sound of Ty's voice came across our two-way radio.

"How far?" asked Proof.

"About five miles straight down the highway," replied Proof.

"Are they Emmonics?"

"No, they don't appear to be."

"Do you want me to send out Springer and Kivi?"

"No," said Ty. "Not yet anyway."

A large group of people became visible tramping down the highway ahead of us in the near distance.

We continued steadily forward down the road. Then one of the strangest things in this entire mission took place. A couple of people from the group ahead of us suddenly broke ranks and dashed rapidly into the flattened cornfield. Kivi and I looked through our military binoculars and saw that they were racing toward what looked like a solitary naked woman standing completely still in the wilderness.

When they reached her an astounding thing happened. A saucer-shaped flying vehicle suddenly darted out of concealment from one of the clouds, swooped down on the two people, sucked them up into the ship by way of a light ray and then shot up into the sky and out of sight within seconds.

"What in the name of Babe Ruth!" I exclaimed.

"Aliens using decoys to gather specimens, would be my guess," Proof said.

"I assume you all saw that," remarked Ty.

"Looks like we have visitors from outer space," Proof told him.

"Not necessarily. Maybe those saucers belong to a more advanced Roselawn-like town."

"No, I still think they're aliens," Proof replied.

"I hope they don't plan on taking over the world," observed Ty.

"Yeah, they probably don't know anything about baseball," joked Proof.

With that bizarre diversion behind us, we resumed our forward journey. The closer we came to the group of people ahead of us the less danger they presented, judging by their condition. There were about thirty of them and they seemed to have just escaped a battle of some type. The Emmonics? Aliens?

"One thing's for sure," Ty reported. "They're definitely Gabrielists. I can see the trumpet in their leader's hands."

Gabrielists belonged to a religious sect which worshipped the Archangel Gabriel. Theirs was a wandering cult which believed that Gabriel was somewhere on the planet, gathering followers to take with him to heaven. The leaders of the sect used trumpets to call out their locations to Gabriel so that he could find them easier. They were known to be harmless and truly deeply religious. It was believed that the trumpets carried by the priests had some form of magical power, being able to freeze people in place when blown at a high enough pitch.

We drove up to the bedraggled group who obviously were not in a disposition to fight. They gathered around our jeeps and we spoke to them from where we sat.

"Looks like you've had a pretty rough time," Ty addressed the long-haired man who was carrying the shiny golden trumpet, the band's leader.

"Yep, we ran into some Bridgers about five miles or so back apiece."

Bridgers were vicious gangs of deformed humans who lived beneath bridges of highway overpasses and cloverleafs. They had a unique ability of camouflage - like chamaeleons - and were able to blend into the environment so they could attack without warning. It was hard to avoid them whenever travelling along a highway.

"Sorry about what happened to you," Ty said. "Is there anything we can do for you?"

"We've got a couple of people with cuts who need some tending to, if you can."

"Sure," said Ty, "we've got some bandages and hydrogen peroxide you can use. None of us are doctors, though."

The injured Gabrielists gathered near the back of Ty's jeep where they got medical supplies from one of the several metal cases we'd brought with us. We then left our seats and mingled and stretched our legs.

Pointing with his trumpet at the rows of robots, the priest asked, "What are those?"

"Robots from the past war," Reggie told him.

"We saw something like them once," the priest said. "But they came out of one of them flying saucer things that had landed."

"We saw a couple of your people get snatched up by a UFO," I told him.

"Yep, we tried to stop them, but they wouldn't listen no how. They thought a person was being crucified out in that field and wanted to save her."

"You must see a lot of strange things wandering down the roads like you do," noted Kivi.

"Probably all there is to see."

"Have you ever seen any living skeletons?" I wondered.

"Yep, a couple of times."

"Really!" I exclaimed. "They're not just a myth?"

"Not unless we was seeing things. But one time it was real sad."

"Sad? Why?" asked Kivi.

"Well, I just happened to blow my instrument of high office in call of Gabriel at the usual hour and some of them skeletons were in the area. The sound made them fall to pieces and drop to the ground."

"That is sad," Kivi replied.

"How about Emmonics?" Reggie wanted to know. "Do you have much trouble with them?"

"Not really. They pretty much leave us alone. I think that they feel we're not too much different from them and so they don't care about us much."

"Have you ever seen their shrine?" Proof asked.

"Nope. We heard tell about it. But never saw it."

"How about their caped men?" Ty asked. "Have you seen any of those guys in the golden capes?"

"Them we have seen." He pointed over his shoulder. "All of them was heading that way - northwest."

"Have you seen any of them recently?" I asked.

"About two weeks ago was the last. He had about a thousand Emmonics following him. There haven't been any since."

"It sounds like maybe the last of them have been gathered up and they're all headed toward the shrine," Proof observed.

The injured Gabrielists finished tending their wounds and it was time for the group to resume their march. Their priest looked to the sun and noted, "It's the hour for the afternoon call."

With that, the others dropped to their knees and bowed their heads. The priest raised his trumpet high and let loose a piercing wail in a high octave. I thought it was a good thing Tina wasn't here because of her sensitive hearing.

The robots were affected by the shrill sound and wavered noticeably instead of hovering steadily as they had been. They resumed normal condition when the priest finished his lengthy trumpet call.

The priest then did the ceremonial ejection of saliva from the horn. Then the ritual was over.

"We can never know if Gabriel heard the call or not," said the priest. "We can only hope and believe that he is even now coming to us with other believers."

"We wish you all the luck in the world," Ty told him.

"Thank you," replied the priest. "And be very careful going ahead. The Bridgers are waiting."

On that note, the Gabrielists started onward the opposite direction down the highway. We too resumed our journey.

"Do you want Kivi and me to check ahead for the Bridgers?" I asked Ty over the two-way.

"No. We know they're out there. You'd only be walking into a trap."

Commanding the robots by his special microphone from inside the jeep, Reggie had them surround us as we continued forward. There didn't seem to be any sign of life of any type as we neared the overpass. The Bridgers could have been anywhere; even in the fields around the roadway they were so perfect at blending in with the surroundings.

"It's just too quiet," noted Proof.

"Yeah, but I don't see a sign of anything anywhere," I replied. "If there are any Bridgers here they must blend right into...everything."

"They're here all right. They already attacked those Gabrielists."

"Well, here comes the overpass. If they're around anywhere we'll know it soon enough."

Then, from nowhere it came. A huge boulder dropped off the edge of the overpass and through the windshield of Ty and Reggie's jeep at the precise moment to send them out of control. Both of them hit their heads and fell unconscious as the jeep swerved forward into a culvert just beyond the overpass.

And the Bridgers pounced. Wild-eyed, bushy-haired, half-naked, inbred maniacs whose only purpose was to kill, destroy and steal what they could. They looked like brawny Neandertals whose only emotion was bloodlust.

The robots continued floating uselessly ahead of us into the distance, no longer under the verbal control of Reggie.

Proof stopped the jeep directly beneath the bridge to avoid any boulders suddenly thrown while the savages rushed both jeeps from all directions.

"Get on the machine gun," Proof yelled to me. "Then I'll pull forward to help the others."

I did as I was instructed and started firing madly at the swarming Bridgers while Kivi fed the belt of bullets into the gun. As I mowed down the charging maniacs,

124

Proof stomped on the gas and we surged forward, just barely avoiding a boulder from above.

Proof stopped an inch from the bumper of the other jeep, leapt out, and lunged into the front seat where he grabbed the microphone that controlled the robots.

I heard him yell the order, "Reverse direction and proceed a hundred yards, emitting stun beams starting at a four-foot-high level off the ground for thirty seconds."

He then waved for Kivi and me to drop low in our seats as he did the same.

The robots obeyed his command and as they returned they felled all of the nearby Bridgers with stun beams. Those in our group were all safe as long as we stayed low.

Once the robots had performed their task and skimmed past, Proof, Kivi and I popped our heads up from cover. At the same time, Reggie and Ty were rising from their short spell of unconsciousness.

"Are you able to drive?" Proof called out to them from his seat.

Both were still groggy. I leapt down from my spot and volunteered to do the driving. There weren't any arguments. Ty retired to the back seat while Reggie slumped in the passenger's seat in the front.

Those Bridgers who'd been biding their time by hiding in the fields now charged us but were still about fifty yards away. Proof then backed his jeep away from mine and I easily got my vehicle out of the culvert.

Soon we were back on the highway, speeding away from the shrieking Bridgers as the squad of robots followed us.

After we'd driven off a safe distance, we parked side by side in the middle of the road.

"Well that was all pretty damn stupid!" Ty shouted over to Reggie.

"You're right. With this robot army we should've been a lot better prepared. We should've just marched through there with stun beams blasting."

I then added, "Well, let's chalk it up as experience and use it against the Emmonics."

"That's a good point," agreed Reggie. "No reason to worry about what we could've done just as long as we don't repeat it."

The excitement over, we headed down the highway and into the undulating Montana countryside, following the steady beep on our tracking device that we hoped led to the Emmonic shrine. For the time being there was nothing around us but the monotony and emptiness of a series of low hills and valleys winding in and out of one another.

11

Birds gracefully winged through a hyacinth blue sky, banking elegantly as if riding the edge of a whirlpool. The air was clear and fresh, exhilarating. The sun was high and bright, scintillating.

I spotted a vast, flower-filled meadow in the middle of which was a tranquil pond adorned with water lilies and on which wild ducks lazily floated. Dragonflies zipped low and crisscrossed again and again above the shiny surface, weaving in and out of the cattails as frogs and turtles watched from shore.

Indecisive butterflies flitted across the meadow from flower to flower, sampling the nectar, while mean-faced badgers rustled through the wiry grass and timid deer looked on from far away.

I peacefully strolled into the breeze-tossed knee-high grass and peered upward at the wind-whisked clouds that streamed in the sky. The air was buzzing with the insects, and the fragrance from the sweet grass and bursting flowers seemed to bathe me in aroma.

Where was this place? How did I get here?

"Hey, what's Springer doing?"

"He seems to be sleeping."

"No, I think it's more than that."

"What do you mean?"

"Here, let me take a look at that bottle?"

"What's wrong?"

"I thought so. He took the wrong bottle and took a pastoral pill instead of a nutrient pill."

"A pastoral pill! What on earth is that?"

"Another invention of mine. When you swallow it you have vivid pastoral hallucinations. It's a great way to escape the ugly, debris-filled ruins of the blasted out areas. The pill's harmless and there aren't any aftereffects."

The breath-taking vision in my mind slowly faded. It was like watching a gorgeous landscape watercolour gradually wash away into a drab blue-grey blur.

"You're wrong about something," I told Reggie when I revived. "There are aftereffects. The world looks a hundred times worse after waking from one of those pills."

"You do have a point."

"How long was I away?" I asked.

"About three hours. You missed lunch. We're just getting ready to get on the road again."

"Okay, I'll take a nutrient pill."

I reached for the bottle but Reggie jerked it away from me, saying, "You better let me get it for you."

I turned out my palm and Reggie dropped a couple of nutrient pills into it.

We prepared to mount our respective vehicles for the day's journey. Before leaving, Ty checked back with Tina in Roselawn to make sure all was well. We also had to keep track of the military satellites and their position so we would know if they were in range should we need to call on their firepower.

Tina was still doing well, but the satellites would not be in position to help us should we need them for another two hours. We didn't know when we would need them; that would be determined by when we located the Emmonic shrine and the situation we faced at that time.

We were now following two signals on our tracking devices. The steady more powerful one we assumed came from the Emmonic shrine. The second signal was a weaker, intermittent one which was coming from the same direction so we assumed that it was somehow related to the shrine. These signals came in the form of radar beeps.

But then there was another sound that was so unexpected that we halted immediately when we heard it. It came from a raised plateau far in the distance and reverberated through the silent air. Tooting! It was a tooting sound.

We instinctively knew what it was even though none of us had ever heard that sound before. In the distance we saw it silhouetted against the wavering blue sky. Chugging along, pouring billows of smoke into the air. It was a railroad train - a very long railroad train jerking and banging through the barren countryside with a great steam locomotive at the head.

"Too bad it's going the opposite direction from us." Ty said. "Otherwise we could hitch a ride."

"Imagine that, a train still operating."

"I wonder if it serves any real purpose," I responded, "or is it just being driven back and forth down the line by a crazed engineer."

"I think that's one of the things we'll have to check on once we're though with the Emmonics," Ty said.

"Yeah." I nodded.

"Okay you train lovers," spoke out Reggie, "let's get this caravan going."

"Right," said Ty.

Onward we rode. Then a different type of sound rushed onto our radios - static. We hadn't gotten any static before because there weren't any radio stations transmitting in the area and the atmosphere was clear of any electrical interference. Where did this noise come from?

We began to follow it and diverted from the road because it was loud and so insistent. We were led over the smooth, rolling land and finally the cause of the crinkly clatter rose up before us.

We gaped at one another in amazement. The vast valley before us was filled with them. Spinning and twirling and seeming to be engaged in a macabre dance. Thousands of skeletons in frenetic motion in various stages of decomposition. Some of them had arms missing, some legs, some heads and other assorted bones.

The wild dancing was without purpose and without consciousness. As they swirled in mad abandon the skeletons spun into one another, filling the air with the clacking sound of their dry bones snapping and cracking as they made contact.

"Well, we found them," sighed Kivi.

"But why here?" asked Proof.

I pointed toward a pulsating yellowish glow coming from behind one of the taller hills in the distance. "Maybe what's causing that pulsing light is what's causing these skeletons to dance."

"You're probably right," Ty said.

"All right, well, let's get going!" cried Reggie.

"Where - right into those skeletons?" asked Kivi.

"Sure. They aren't going to feel anything," Reggie responded."

"I want to walk," Kivi said.

"What!" said Proof.

"Me, too," I agreed.

Ty gave us his typical wave of the hand in agreement. "These two need some exercise," he told the others, "they've been sitting too long. That's not good for major league field scouts. Besides, I would like them to have a look ahead."

Kivi and I leapt from our seats and plunged head long into the field filled with magnetised skeletons. It was the eeriest experience of my life. All around me were skeletons. Dancing, spinning, swirling; some had sardonic grins, some had their entire mouths missing, some their heads. As they spun and twirled it seemed like they were reaching for me, trying to communicate with the. Call for help even.

The touch of their bony fingers made me shiver. Peering into their deadened eye sockets - those that still had them - struck me to the gut. And I'm sure that Kivi felt the same, judging by her expression of terror and amazement.

There was something else very bizarre in the middle of this valley. The air was alive with electricity; I could feel it crawling all over me as if I were covered by ants. It made my ears hot and caused them to violently ring. And I could hear the sound of the electromagnetic energy like a constant buzzing in the air.

It was obviously being caused by an incredibly powerful electromagnetic source which was just beyond the hill.

Kivi and I were alerted by the sound of the jeep horn's blaring. Looking backward we saw that they had detoured and were going around the rim of the valley. The robots were accompanying them.

Kivi and I waved and then resumed forward at a quicker pace.

"Why do you suppose they're going around?" Kivi asked.

"The electromagnetic waves are messing up the jeeps' engines. Probably affecting the robots, too."

"I feel like sprinting," Kivi told me. "I'm going to go ahead."

"I'd like to speed it up, too. Let's go."

Kivi sped off ahead. As I jogged forward through the throngs of skeletons I was once again struck by that otherworldly feeling I'd sometimes get while in the open alone.

This time it was particularly curious because the sight of the valley filled with skeletons was interchanged with quick flashes of crowds of fully formed people standing erect and motionless, staring toward the sky. Back and forth this vision changed several times before I was left with the one present reality. By that time, I had reached the end of the field of skeletons.

I re-joined Kivi on the slope that led out of the valley. At the same time the jeeps circled the rim of the valley and met us on the middle of the hillside with the robots near.

We stood silent as a group staring up to the crest of the rise, watching the sky on the other side throb with a golden glow. Without a word, Ty started his jeep forward first and the two vehicles bucked over the ridge while Kivi and I made the long leaping steps forward. The robots followed behind and Reggie had them assume a position in a line atop the hill.

Before us was a vast plain. It was filled with white-robed Emmonics but they were so far distant that they were but specks of movement in the grey-blue grasslands. We could only hear a faint murmur of sound.

At the opposite end of the plain from us was the great Emmonic shrine, standing alone and spectacular; a bullet-shaped, dull bronze coloured structure of enormous size, almost touching the low cloud tops.

"Look at the size of that thing!" gasped Kivi.

"I can't believe the Emmonics could've built that," I observed.

"It's probably leftover from the war," Reggie remarked.

"See that ground below us," Ty said. "That's where Custer made his last stand on June 25, 1876. Want to know something really ironic? On the day that Custer was being massacred in the West, several teams of the newly created National Baseball league were playing their schedule in the East?"

"Looks like instead of Indians we've got a few thousand Emmonics waiting for us," noted Proof.

"And this won't be no baseball game," responded Reggie.

"I don't know if even those robots of yours will be able to melt that shrine," Ty said to Reggie.

"The satellites might be able to carve them down."

"The trouble is they won't be in range for another half hour."

"And I don't think we have a half hour to wait," I said, then pointed toward the Emmonics. "I think they've spotted us."

"You're right," said Ty. "And they're not waiting for us to come to them. They're already marching on us."

Three Masters of Divine Hearing were leading the way. The glowing we'd seen had come from the capes of the Masters' which were blazing with energy probably transmitted from the shrine.

"Looks like we'll have to fight them on their terms," said Ty.

"We're ready," said Kivi.

"No, I have something a lot more important for you two to do," Ty told us. He then removed a couple of white robes that he'd been concealing in the back of the jeep. "I want you to put these on, pretend to be Emmonics, and get to that shrine and find out all you can about it."

"Good idea, Ty," Proof said. "We may not even make it. But these two in disguise will have a really good chance."

Reggie then took out one of his scientific creations and handed it to me. "Take this with you. It's a directional device that works automatically. I've got it set to directly contact the tracking centre in Roselawn so the satellites can have a target to aim at. Just drop it somewhere in the middle of the plain. It's made of hard metal and will withstand a lot"

"Right," I said, taking it.

Kivi and I slipped on the robes then each of us hid in separate jeeps so we could jump out at the right time and blend in with the Emmonics.

The jeeps and robots started down into the madness. At first both sides were cautious in approaching each other. Then the three Masters of Divine Hearing thrust their staffs skyward. The air reverberated with the horrific shout made by the Emmonics as one voice as they charged forward.

Reggie placed the robots in a long line in front of us and unleashed them. We followed at a safe distance behind the robots, Proof manning a machine gun and Reggie dipping his hand into a case of explosives.

Then disaster struck. A sheet of electromagnetic energy was generated from the capes of the Masters of Divine hearing and engulfed the line of robots, instantly draining them of power. They all dropped dead in their tracks.

The Emmonics surged forward. Our jeeps forged into them. Kivi and I leapt out simultaneously at the moment of contact and were lost in the flurry of action.

The sound of white robes flapping in the wind and razor sharp cleavers being drawn and ringing against one another swirled all around us as we rolled madly amidst the chaos. No one seemed to notice that we'd flung ourselves from the jeeps, probably because we'd been smothered in the thick clouds of dust and smoke that the grinding tires of the vehicles had heaved into the air.

I twisted to my feet and saw Reggie heave one of his sheets directly onto the cape of one of the Masters of Divine Hearing. It was the same caped man who had killed Gelp so long ago.

The Master was buried under the already flaming atomic sheet, spinning madly in an unsuccessful attempt to fling it off him. The Emmonics fled from him as he sprayed blazing sparks in a fiery shower while he flailed and twirled and roasted. As he gradually incinerated,

Reggie leapt from his jeep and jumped into Ty's place where he manned the machine gun.

Kivi and I watched as Ty sped toward a second one of the Masters of Divine Hearing. She and I raced to the spot, too, but not sure why. Our plans had abruptly changed.

The Master aimed his staff at the jeep. I hurled the homing device at the Master's head. It stung him sharply in the temple, dropping him to the ground, sending his staff flying wildly skyward. I caught it. At the same time, Kivi yanked off the Master's cape.

Enraged Emmonics swarmed toward Kivi and me. I found that the staff was controlled by a set of buttons on its side. Pressing one of the buttons, I set loose an invisible force from one end of the staff which flattened anything in front of me to the ground like a mighty gust of wind would.

Ty roared the jeep over to Kivi and me and we both leapt in. With Reggie blasting away with the machine gun and me felling anything in our path we bounded over sprawled bodies and rugged terrain toward the Emmonic shrine with the demonic horde pursuing us.

The Emmonics weren't all on foot. Many of them had driven to the shrine in vehicles and they came after us in them. It was just a matter of time before we were overrun.

We had one hope - the satellites.

Ty shouted over to Reggie, "Check with Roselawn."

"Right."

Ty then shouted to me, "Where's the directional homing device?"

"Back there." I pointed. "I knocked the caped guy unconscious with it."

"Just as well," said Ty.

"Two of the satellites are in range," Reggie announced. "The other five won't be for another fifteen to twenty-five minutes."

"Have them all start firing the minute they come in range," Ty ordered. "Use the tracking marker as the target and blast everything in a two-mile circumference around it."

"Right. My thinking exactly."

Reggie gave the order. Then he, Kivi and I sat down and grabbed hold as hard as we could as Ty made a mad rush toward the shrine. We weren't sure why he was speeding so madly toward the shrine since it was in the centre of the targeted area. But Ty always had a good

141

reason for what he did. That was his managerial talent; thinking several moves ahead. None was better at it than Ty.

The satellite attack began. Bolt after bolt of sizzling laser light struck the ground, throwing heaps of dirt and rock and tangles of dead Emmonics into the air. Again and again and again the beams blasted into the ground, tearing out chasms and boring hot, steaming craters into the pulverised earth.

The Emmonics abandoned their hunting of us. They frantically sprinted and sped in their vehicles toward the rim of the valley, leaving hundreds of cast off cleavers glinting in the sunlight where they lay on the ground.

The assault from the sky became even fiercer when the other satellites came into range. The ground was slammed by a constant barrage of explosions and the air was stung without stop by shots of laser light.

Closer and closer we came to the shrine. So did the attacks from above as they seemed to be following us. There were only a few random strikes in front of us, which I believed was pure chance.

Several bolts struck the shrine and tore long slash marks down the exterior, exploding with immense force at the base of the edifice. And that's where Ty headed - one of the points at the bottom of the shrine where the ground had been blasted away.

Through the storm of laser light we raced until finally stopping at the edge of a trench which had been cut into the ground at the base of the shrine.

Ty pointed to a shallow slice that had been seared into the metal surface, shouting, "That's where we go in."

"Go in!" cried Proof. "How? Why?"

"Why? Because we have to," Ty told him. "How? Reggie's material."

"Good!" glowed Reggie. "A test of my material's strength. Good!"

It was clear what we had to do. Only a scratch had been made in the surface, showing how strong the material was that made up the shrine. But that scratch gave us an opening into the interior of the metal and it was in this opening that one of Reggie's atomic sheets would be stuffed.

Reggie contacted Roselawn and had the bombardment stop since the Emmonics were no longer chasing us. But we were still in great danger. The Emmonics probably would return and the satellites would soon be back out of range.

We had to act quickly. The five of us leapt out of the jeep and Reggie whipped a sheet from his case and stuffed it into the five-inch-deep, three-inch-wide, six-foot-long tear in the shrine's wall. The burning was intense, and we all stood back from the stifling heat.

"Are we sure that there aren't any doors of some type built into this thing?" I asked.

"You know, that's a really good question," Ty said. "There may very well be."

"What if Kivi and I took a run around the base of the shrine - she going one way and me the other - to find out, and meet back here?" I suggested.

"Another good thought," said Ty. "I think you might have manager material, Springer."

"I think I might make a better pitcher," I told him.

"Why is that?"

"I knocked that caped man cold with that directional tracking thing I threw at him earlier."

"Yeah, that was quite a throw," Kivi vouched for me.

"Well for right now," Proof interjected, "let's just see how good of a door finder you are."

"Right," I said. I then gave Kivi a pat on the shoulder and the two of us were off in opposite directions.

There were two reasons we didn't take the jeep. One of them was that the ground around the base of the shrine had been too torn up by the satellite blasts to drive on. The other reason was because the radio was in the jeep and the others might need to contact Roselawn with it.

After only a few strides I was completely alone with the gigantic curved wall of the shrine on my right. The silence was extreme. The monstrous shrine blocked out any sounds from behind it and around it, and the plain which moments ago had been a battlefield was completely deserted.

But then the silence was suddenly pricked. I heard a high pitched insistent whining sound that was like the whistle of a boiling tea kettle. It wasn't loud, though. It was whiny and continuous and it was coming from the wall of the shrine.

I stopped. Testing the wall of the shrine with my palm, I felt it to be slightly vibrating. I put an ear close to the metal and heard a ringing sound. Could it be that the laser strikes had cause the structure to shiver like a bell?

Leaving that mystery to take back to Ty and the others, I resumed my lope around the shrine. There were not any doors or openings of any type in the amazingly smooth, dull metallic surface. There wasn't a nick or a flaw on the metal except those placed into it by the lasers.

I met Kivi about halfway around the base and then returned to where the others were. We found them gathered around the radio while a second of Reggie's atomic sheets was melting deeper into the thick metal.

"What're you doing?" I asked.

"Listen," said Ty, pointing me toward the radio's speaker.

I listened. It was the sound of thousands upon thousands upon thousands of human voices all shouting together at the same time so that all you really could hear was a high-pitched ringing like a tape recorder being rewound at rapid speed.

I stood back. "You know, that reminds me of something."

"What?" Ty asked.

I pointed toward the shrine and told them, "Like the sound coming from the wall of the shrine that I heard while I was going around it. Somehow, it's being picked up as radio waves on the receiver."

"That makes sense," replied Reggie. "I thought I heard a ringing coming from the wall when I was placing my second sheet in the opening."

"But...what does it mean?" asked Kivi.

"This is only a guess," Reggie replied, "But I think that those sounds on the shrine's wall and on the radio are the voices of millions of people screaming in horror at the moment they were incinerated by nuclear explosions. Somehow they were imbedded into the metal of the shrine like on one of Edison's first metal tape recording cylinders."

"That makes sense," said Ty.

"It's really sad," moaned Kivi.

"It's only a guess, remember," said Reggie.

"A pretty good one, I'd say," remarked Proof.

"It's all interesting," responded Ty, "but it's probably nothing compared to what we'll find inside the shrine."

"Right," said Proof, "and we better keep working at it before the Emmonics come back."

"And I'm sure they will be coming," Ty replied. "There's still one of those Masters of Divine Hearing running loose out there."

"He'll probably round up the surviving Emmonics and bring them back after us."

For one of the few times, I spoke directly to Reggie, asking him, "I was wondering, do you think we might be able to reactivate the robots?"

His eyes widened with the sudden idea. "Hey! That might be possible. But I'd have to go out to where they're disabled and check on them."

"I think you should," said Ty. "I have a feeling the Emmonics will be back and we'll need the robots. Take the jeep."

"I'll go with him," said Proof. "He can drop me off at the other jeep and we'll have both of them back."

"Good idea," agreed Ty. "And we'll burn the rest of the way into the shrine...I hope."

Reggie and Proof leapt into the jeep and Kivi, Ty and me focused on getting into the shrine.

12

Peering into the side of the shrine where the atomic sheet was blazing was like looking into the radiance of the sun, something you did not do for long.

"This is almost the end of the burning cycle of the second sheet." Ty told us.

"How long is a burning cycle?"

"Hard to say. At the start it took a full eight minutes for the first sheet to burn out because it was going through un-softened metal."

"Un-softened metal?" asked Kivi.

"Metal that hadn't felt any burning yet. But the second sheet burned out in six minutes - or is about to - because the metal was already heated and softened."

"How deep has it penetrated so far?" I asked.

"I'd gauge about six feet. I can't believe this thing is much thicker than that. Can you imagine how much metal was used to build this?"

Kivi picked up the cape from the Master of Divine Hearing that she'd earlier ripped from the man and said, "I had a thought. They were able to direct a lot of power through this cape - from the shrine I guess - is there some way we can do that, too?"

"Why didn't we think of that!" exclaimed Ty. You're right, Kivi! I'll bet that the cape can be controlled with the staff."

"Let's give it a test," I said, picking up the staff from where I'd laid it.

"What...do I do?" asked Kivi.

"For right now," Ty said, "just lay the cape on the ground. Then Springer can go through the controls on the staff and see what happens."

Kivi spread the cape on the ground and I fingered the three buttons. When I pressed the top and the bottom of the three buttons the cape began to brilliantly glow and send out a powerful electromagnetic force field. It threw the three of us back against the wall of the shrine.

We were suddenly distracted by gunfire from the distance. Reggie and Proof had contacted the Emmonics and were fighting them off. We saw a lone jeep bucking across the torn up ground toward us followed by a horde of cleaver-swinging Emmonics led by one of the Masters of Divine Hearing.

"Here come the Emmonics again!" shouted Kivi.

"Proof and Reggie couldn't make it to the robots," Ty noted, viewing them with his telescopic sight.

The Jeep with Proof and Reggie skidded up to us far ahead of the Emmonics. They saw us experimenting with the cape and staff of the Master of Divine Hearing.

"It's easy to see that you didn't make out too well," Ty said to Proof and Reggie.

"No, there're still hundreds of them out there," replied Reggie. "And they'll be on us before the satellites come back into range."

"We've been working with this cape and staff we took from one of those Masters of Divine Hearing," I said. "We may be able to use them."

"Let's see," said Proof, leaping from the jeep.

Proof then unfurled the cape over his shoulders and took the staff.

"You can get power from the cape by using the buttons on the staff." I told him.

"All right, let's see," said Proof, experimenting.

Pointing the staff before him like a weapon, Proof got several effects from it, one of which was to be able to tear a huge crevice in the ground with a sweep of the staff. Just like the Emmonic caped man once did to us, causing our vehicle to plummet into the ground.

"That's it!" cried Proof.

He then leapt back into the jeep and instructed Reggie to rush toward the nearing Emmonics. Reggie understood the plan and raced forward.

At this point, Kivi, Ty and I could only watch. And it was an inspiring, though deadly, sight to behold.

The two sides charged toward each other with complete abandon. Just before they met, Reggie jammed the jeep to a sudden stop, Proof leapt onto the hood and directed the staff at the ground just like the Master of Divine Hearing had done to us. A swath was torn into the earth a quarter mile long and an eighth mile deep and the Emmonics piled into it in droves.

The Emmonics who remained on the other side of the chasm were machine-gunned by Reggie after he turned around the vehicle. It was magnificent carnage!

I could say that in retrospect because our victory was not complete. There was one survivor of the Emmonics and that was the third Master of Divine Hearing.

He had the ability to levitate and he floated across the chasm to face Proof. The two men stood within a few yards of each other in what was like a bizarre Wild West showdown. Each man fired point blank at the other and both men were incinerated. There was nothing left of either of them except a patch of smoke which rose skyward then dissipated.

Even Reggie was shocked. After several minutes, he headed back toward us, obviously saddened by the loss.

We'd now lost our three best friends and three best baseball players: Gelp, Ulfson and now Proof. Although the whereabouts of Ulfson was still uncertain.

We were all silent when Reggie reached our position, and we quietly returned to burning our way into the shrine. Ty had placed the third atomic sheet within the widening crack and it seared through the metal much more quickly than the others, finally, breaking through to the other side.

We scooped handful after handful of dirt into the opening to cool down the molten metal and make it possible for us to enter. Then at last we were ready to enter the shrine, having just barely enough room by which to squeeze inside.

"In honour of Proof," Reggie said.

153

"Gelp and Ulfson, too," I added.

"Quite right, Springer," agreed Ty.

"Who should lead the way?" asked Kivi.

"Reggie, I'd say," replied Ty. "We couldn't have gotten in without his material."

Reggie nodded respectfully and silently started into the narrow slit opening.

13

All of us had to slide in sideways in single file to get into the shrine. Reggie led the way, dragging his case of sheets with him, followed by Kivi, Ty, then me. It seemed strange that there were only four of us left.

We entered the shrine and found it to be in the form of a gigantic multi-level shopping centre complete with criss-crossing escalators and numerous elevators. A florescent type of artificial lighting came directly from the walls and ceiling, bathing everything in a pinkish/white glow.

There wasn't any sign of human life. But there was another type of life: mechanical.

Seconds after we set foot in the vast complex we were accosted by a ten-foot-tall, sledgehammer-headed robot with multiple arms that were like long spears.

"You are in a restricted area," spoke the robot in a very sluggish voice as if its batteries were badly run down. "You must be taken to the high counsellor for determination."

"What does that mean?" Ty asked it.

The robot did not reply but extended an arm to its right, saying, "Go that way."

"What if we don't?" I asked it.

"You will be rendered unconscious by the emission of toxic gases."

"We'll follow instructions," said Ty, giving me a wink.

The lumbering robot led us from the main plaza down a long, darkly lit corridor. The hallway was littered with several human skeletons, some of whom were lying with their fingers pressed against the wall that led directly to the outer wall. The wall was scarred with long scratch marks.

"What do you make of it?" I asked no one in particular.

"They were scratching on the walls to get out," Kivi instantly replied. "Some of them died doing it."

"I'd say she's right," agreed Reggie.

"This way," said the much-depleted robot.

It led us around a widely curving corner which opened directly onto a spacious circular room whose walls were filled with computers and monitor screens. Many of the monitors were still operating and gave views into various other locations throughout this vast complex. There still wasn't any sign of living human occupants.

Among the places shown on the monitors were small movie theatres, cafes, gyms and personal residences. This seemed to have been a well-designed habitat. But by who, and what happened to the inhabitants?

In the centre of the room was a semi-circular desk behind which was seated a fully clothed skeleton. This was the high counsellor.

The robot addressed the high counsellor, "Sir, I apprehended these four individuals in a restricted zone. They were in the centre portion of the New World Edifice and were not displaying the proper badges."

The robot waited for a reply that of course was not forthcoming.

Ty addressed the robot. "Your high counsellor is dead - just a bunch of bones!"

"Nonetheless, I must await his orders."

"How can a dead man give you orders?" Ty questioned.

"I cannot respond to that."

"Isn't there someone else you can speak to about us?" I asked the robot.

"Affirmative. The vice high counsellor in the event the high counsellor is incapacitated."

"Then speak to the vice high counsellor," I said.

"I have not as yet been given official notification that the high counsellor is incapacitated."

"He's dead!" cried Reggie. "He can't be any more incapacitated than that!"

"I still require official notification of that fact."

"Let's play his game," Reggie suggested.

"What do you mean?" Ty asked.

"While the robot waits for a response from the skeleton, let's just go about our business. All that he was instructed to do was remove us from the restricted area. It's like any other mindless machine. It can't think independently."

"Good idea," said Ty. "Let's take a look around this place then."

So, while the robot waited for instructions from the skeleton in the seat, we started toward the door. But we suddenly stopped. A computerised voice from nowhere began speaking to us.

"You have activated the automatic replay system. Stand by for a vital visual and audio message from the high counsellor."

"This should be interesting," Reggie noted with sarcasm.

A five-foot-by-five-foot video screen lowered from the ceiling and blinked on. The figure of a tall, thin woman wearing the same uniform in which the skeleton was dressed appeared on the screen. We all froze before it. Then the voice came from the wall speakers.

"Before I begin, I would like to inform you that this system is interactive - you may ask questions - and you may give verbal commands to stop or start this recording or even to replay a passage as you desire.

"I am Arla, the leader of this failed community. I am sorry that I can only greet you as an image on a screen. We will all surely be dead by the time that anyone finds a way inside our New World Edifice.

"This great monstrosity in which you now find yourselves was constructed by a collection of scientific geniuses encompassing all of the disciplines. We knew that nuclear war was inevitable and escaped inside here to wait out the holocaust.

"It was our intention to emerge once it was safe and then to rebuild civilisation. But our society within these walls, also went mad and destroyed itself as well."

"The war ended over two hundred years ago," Ty addressed the computer image, "did you ever emerge from this structure?"

"No, we did not," the reply came. "We were unable to. Our structure sustained many nuclear strikes and, although being able to survive destruction, we found that the nuclear bombardment altered the very atomic structure of the metal that the edifice was made of. The seams of our dome were welded shut in such a way that we could not open them to escape as we had planned to."

"You mean that none of you were able to get out?" asked Kivi.

"There were legends that a few escaped through a secret exit. These remain legends. We were never able to devise any type of explosive or spring mechanism that could free us all from this prison."

"Are you aware of any government on this planet that created an army of doomsday robots that would destroy any survivors of the nuclear war?" Reggie wanted to know.

"We were unaware of any such enterprise."

There was a pause. And when no other questions were forthcoming, the computer image resumed its talk.

"Since we were unable to manually free ourselves we decided to seek outside assistance. We converted our entire citadel into a high-powered transmitter of microwave emissions. We sent these signals to all directions in the hopes of penetrating the minds of any survivors and attracting them here to save us. No one ever came, or, if they did, couldn't help us. If you are here now and hearing this message it is obvious that in some way we succeeded, but too late to be of any help to us."

"Then you all would have died by either starvation or dehydration - or mass suicide," I said to the computer.

"You are correct. The choice was left to the individual. Most people chose to wait until help arrived, and died waiting.

"There is nothing more to tell. It is hoped that you will be able to use the technology of our edifice and in this way help advance civilisation. Any technical questions you have can be answered through the computers at our technical control centre which is cell TTC111."

The voice concluded, the image disappeared and the video screen rose back upward into the ceiling.

"The Emmonics," said Ty, "were brought here by microwaves - whatever those are."

"I guess only certain people are affected by them," I noted.

We were all shocked by a sudden piercing scream. Each of us threw a stunned expression to the other.

"No, it can't be a survivor," Ty answered everyone's question.

"Then...who?" asked Kivi.

"Emmonics!" replied Reggie.

"I give them credit," I replied, "they don't give up."

"We have to stop them once and for all," spoke Ty.

"Right," said Reggie. "We have to shut off that microwave transmitter."

"How?" asked Kivi.

"Go to room TTC111 like the voice directed us," I told her.

"There was a map of the complex near where we entered," said Ty. "Let's get some directions."

We hurried back to the main concourse. According to the schematic, the room we wanted was straight upward and reachable directly by an elevator in a central tube. As we rushed toward the elevator we were spotted by a group of about ten Emmonics. They closed in on us fast!

Ty pointed toward Kivi and me and made a sweeping motion. We both knew what that meant - distract the Emmonics, then return to the elevator.

While Ty and Reggie made for the elevator - slowed by Reggie's bad leg - Kivi and I sped off in what would be a long, looping circle around the spacious concourse. All of the Emmonics followed us. And, just as planned, we opened a large lead on them, so that when Kivi and I circled back to the elevator they were far behind, their shrieking echoing off the walls.

Ty and Reggie were waiting for us at the elevator's opened doors and we joined them inside without any more trouble. The circular compartment was sucked up the tube so fast that I believe our feet actually left the floor. Fortunately, it eased to a comfortable stop at the very apex of the gigantic dome.

We exited into a vast, circular room whose walls, even though solid, were transparent and gave us an unobstructed view of the land and the sky around the dome. It was breath-taking! I was not the only one with my mouth agape as I looked out at the world around us.

And then we saw something that was even more astounding! Two flying saucer shaped vehicles appeared in the sky and swooped low over the battlefield, apparently scanning it. When they were done with that, they flew toward the dome, circled it a couple of times and then hovered near the top, one on each side of the structure.

Could they see us peering out at them? Could they somehow sense we were there? What did they want?

"The microwaves," I said. "Maybe they're attracted to them."

Reggie was studying a console filled with dials and switches and buttons. "Well," he said, "let's see what happens when I shut off the transmitter."

He threw the switch. Both saucers drew closer to the citadel, almost touching it. Then the shortwave radio in the edifice, which was in a constant state of receiving, was suddenly flooded with a gush of messages in a variety of languages. One of them was English. Reggie separated it out from the others.

"We have come in response to your call for help," was the message from the saucer. "Our craft was in the vicinity of your planet when we heard your call."

"What do we tell them?" Ty asked.

"A brief history of our world," I suggested.

Reggie nodded. He picked up the microphone and gave this response, "Our world was devastated by nuclear war about two centuries ago. We are no longer in need of assistance.”

“Understood,” was the reply. “We will register your planet as inhabited by sentient beings and schedule future exploratory visits. We can maintain materialization for only seconds. Must now depart.”

“We will await your future return.”

With that, the radio became silent. Both saucers vertically rose about fifty feet, then vanished in a flash.

“Hey, what about the Emmonics!” exclaimed Kivi.

We peered below and saw that the Emmonics who had been chasing us were now wandering around the floor of the dome, seemingly very confused.

“They aren’t under the influence of the microwaves any longer,” Reggie said. “I’ll bet they’re pretty tame now.”

“Let’s go introduce ourselves,” suggested Ty.

Reggie reached into his case and gave each of us a stun bomb, just in case the Emmonics weren’t so tame.

14

Reggie remained in the control centre while Ty, Kivi and I rode down to the ground floor on the elevator. We weren't sure what to expect, but from above the Emmonics seemed to be more bewildered than combative. Who knows, maybe they would greet us a gods!

The elevator door opened and we stepped out. There was a group of Emmonics waiting for us. One of them stepped forward, bowing as he said with trembling voice, "Are...are you the angelic messengers of the God Blasteron?"

"Those days are over," Ty cautiously told him.

"I...I hardly remember anything of the old days," said the Emmonic. The others behind him shook their heads in agreement.

"A lot of senseless killing," another Emmonic replied.

"That's all over now," I told them. "This is where the new world begins."

"Well said," Ty told me. "Very well said."

Extra Innings

It was finally all over. Now we could get back to playing baseball. Reggie remained in the dome where he took control of things.

People began to journey to the citadel from all over the country in search of a new place to live. It wasn't like the holy pilgrimage of the Emmonics.

None of the Emmonics were under the influence of the microwaves any longer and those who survived became useful citizens of the new civilisation.

Reggie was able to mass produce much larger copies of his atomic sheets and soon vast areas of land were freed of debris and were put under cultivation.

Ty, Kivi and I returned to Roselawn with Reggie's robots repaired and now under our control. They would provide a valuable army in the future should we ever need one.

We turned Roselawn into the baseball capital of the country and established our new team there. Travel was still important to spread news and culture so we still went on road trips.

Proper memorials were made for both Gelp and Proof. And there was one joyous discovery to announce. When we put together our new team it was with our old first baseman playing at his former position.

Ulfson! On our trip back to Roselawn we found Ulfson hiking down one of the roads. During the attack that cost us our catcher, Ulfson had been knocked senseless and had wandered off into the wilderness. Now he was back with us and in excellent playing condition.

The schedule was set for our new baseball league and it was time to PLAY BALL!

the end

wtwtw